WHAT YOU PROPOSE

ANYTHING FOR LOVE - BOOK 2

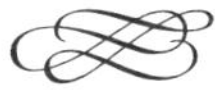

ADELE CLEE

This is a work of fiction. All names, characters, places and incidents are products of the author's imagination. All characters are fictitious. Any resemblance to real persons, living or dead, is purely coincidental.

ISBN-13: 978-0-9935291-1-5

Cover designed by **Jay Aheer**

Books by Adele Clee

To Save a Sinner

A Curse of the Heart

What Every Lord Wants

The Secret To Your Surrender

A Simple Case of Seduction

Anything for Love Series

What You Desire

What You Propose

What You Deserve

What You Promised

The Brotherhood Series

Lost to the Night

Slave to the Night

Abandoned to the Night

Lured to the Night

Lost Ladies of London

The Mysterious Miss Flint

The Deceptive Lady Darby

The Scandalous Lady Sandford

The Daring Miss Darcy

Avenging Lords

At Last the Rogue Returns

CHAPTER 1

A VILLAGE NORTHEAST OF SAINT-BRIEUC, FRANCE, 1820

Marcus Danbury raced through the cloisters, the clip of his boots echoing along the ancient corridors.

"Tristan." He stormed through the arched doorway out into the courtyard. The usually peaceful recreation area provided little comfort today. "Tristan!"

Where the bloody hell had he got to?

Marcus placed his fists on his hips as he scanned the row of small windows set into the stone wall. He would wager twenty gold francs his friend still lay snoring in his bed.

They had drunk far too much wine last night. So much so, Marcus had been forced to dunk his head into the gardener's barrel in the hope the cold water would waken his numb brain.

Despite his frustration, he had to chuckle at the irony of his situation.

One would expect a monastery to be a haven from the trials and temptations of loose women. Who would ever have thought he'd offer sanctuary to the madam of a bawdy house? Although he hadn't exactly offered to play host; the request had been more akin to bribery, and he'd had less than a day's notice to get used to the idea. Had it not been for the debt he owed to the Marquess of Danesfield, he would storm down to the rusty gate and inform Dane's coachman to turn around and take the strumpet straight back to England.

An image of a well-rounded woman with a huge powdered wig and heavily rouged cheeks flashed into his mind. She would have a fake mole, of course, close to the lips, which would alter in size depending on how drunk she was when she applied it. No doubt her generous bosom would be bursting out from the strict confines of her dress, wobbling and jiggling about when she walked, just to torment him.

God, it had been weeks since he'd last settled between a pair of soft thighs, which was why he supposed he should be grateful to Dane. After numerous years in service, he was confident this Madame Labelle possessed all the necessary skills needed when it came to giving pleasure. Should her countenance be so dreadfully unappealing, he would just have to close his eyes.

"Tristan."

The sound of a window opening caught his attention, and he spotted a mop of golden hair and a pair of beady eyes peering out of the tiny gap.

"What is it?" Tristan shouted, his bare arm hanging from the handle. Clearly he had only just dragged himself out of bed.

"The carriage is waiting at the gate."

"What carriage?"

"Madame Labelle's or Miss Labelle's or whatever the hell her name is."

In his letter, Dane mentioned the woman had been in partnership with a Frenchman yet they'd never married. In the eyes of the Lord, she must be as good as wed to a hundred men. Marcus shook his head. Hypocrisy was a trait he despised; no one deemed him virtuous or moral and so he could hardly cast aspersions. Indeed, he had often wondered if living in an abandoned monastery was a form of penance.

Tristan opened the window fully. “So why haven’t you sent someone down to let her in?”

“I thought you could go.”

Most of the servants had gone to the market and on Thursdays Andre distributed alms in the village. Selene would be busy in the kitchen, and he’d be damned if he’d go.

In London, Madame Labelle might be the ruler of her domain, but he refused to pander to her whims. Here, she would answer to him. Here, he was the master and as such he refused to do anything to weaken his position—including acting as the hired help.

Madame Labelle could sit in her carriage for the rest of the day for all he cared.

Perhaps living in a monastery might provide enlightenment, might make her reconsider her disreputable ways. To be virtuous, one must first learn patience. Thirty minutes sitting in a stationary carriage would certainly help her do that.

“Give me a few minutes.” Tristan sighed. “I need to dress.”

“There might be a reward in it.” Marcus chuckled to himself.

One look at Tristan’s handsome features and the bawd would be offering to pay him for his services, although he had yet to see Tristan succumb to any woman. He didn’t hold out much hope for a haggard, middle-aged matron of a brothel.

After waiting for fifteen minutes, Tristan met him in the chapter house. Marcus had stripped away all decorative objects and used the room as a study, a library, and a private sanctuary.

“Perhaps it is wise I do go down and let them in,” Tristan said, scanning Marcus’ relaxed attire. “You do realise your shirt is wet around the collar, and your breeches look as though a donkey has slept on them. Will you not at least wear a coat?”

“No. This Madame Labelle creature can take me as she finds me.” He brushed his hand through his hair in a bid to tame the wild, unruly locks. After spending years servicing the aristocracy, the woman would probably find him rather crude and uncouth. The thought pleased him greatly, and he snorted with amusement.

"Well, she will find you have the clothes of a beggar and the look of a libertine."

"Good." He waved his hand down the front of his friend's fitted coat and pristine cravat. "You will more than make up for my inferior apparel and shoddy manners."

Tristan chuckled. "Did Dane tell you why he's sent her here?"

"He was somewhat vague. He said the woman offered him assistance."

"I'm sure she did."

"He wants to keep her out of London for a while."

"Yes, but for how long?"

Marcus shrugged. "I have no idea. But if she's staying here, she can damn well earn her keep."

Tristan's eyes grew wide. "You don't mean to—"

"I mean she can work in the kitchen," he interjected with a grin. "She will learn that there are no airs and graces here. She cannot flash her fleshy wares in the hope of securing a warm bed and a hot meal for the evening. If she wants to eat, she works. Just as we all do."

"Andre could do with some help in the garden."

Marcus grabbed his friend's shoulder. "Well, there you have it. Madame Labelle will be the new gardener. We shall see if the woman's fingers are as nimble as her profession demands."

Marcus spent the next ten minutes pacing the floor. A strange feeling settled in his chest. The woman's presence would create a shift, unsettle the equilibrium; it would involve them all making changes, certain allowances. She may have experience running a bawdy house, but she would play no part in running his house.

Should he greet her at the door, let her feel the sharpness of his tongue, let her know of his indifference to her plight? Should he sit behind his large desk, busy scratching away with a quill pen and ink and pay her no heed?

Damn it.

He could hear the carriage wheels rattling over the stone bridge.

Madame Labelle needed to feel the weight of his authority. She needed to know he would not tolerate any interference.

With that in mind, he strode out through the cloisters and crossed the garth to the entrance located in the west wing. With the bar already raised, Marcus pushed the reinforced oak doors just as the carriage rumbled to a halt outside. His gaze darted to the box seat of the conveyance, to see Tristan perched on top sporting a wide grin.

"Look who's here," Tristan cried with genuine excitement.

As the coachman removed his hat, Marcus sucked in a breath. "Haines." He rushed forward. "By God, I'm surprised Dane sent you. How was your journey?"

Marcus expected him to raise a weary brow and offer a grim expression as he jerked his head towards the carriage.

"It was a good crossing," he said, without showing the slightest sign of irritation. "Spent the time playing cards and supping too much ale. The lady kept to her cabin, mostly. I don't think the motion suited her stomach if you take my meaning."

More like she'd decided to earn a few guineas and used sickness as an excuse to stay abed.

"How long will you stay with us?"

"Only for a day or two. Just until the lady's all settled."

Marcus could not recall a time when he'd heard a man refer to a whore as a lady. Haines was probably just being polite. The man had a heart as large as his stocky frame. Either that or he had developed a *tendre* for the woman during the journey.

"Talking of which," Tristan said. "I should get down and help her out."

Tristan wore a smug grin. Or perhaps Marcus was mistaken.

Perhaps his friend was simply pleased to be reunited with the man who had once saved both their lives.

Marcus took a few steps back, squared his shoulders and raised his chin. He may dress as a peasant, but he knew how to convey the countenance of a duke.

Tristan opened the carriage door and let down the steps before offering his hand to the occupant.

As Madame Labelle descended the three tiny steps with all the demureness of a duchess, Marcus almost expired from a distinct lack of air. He sucked in a breath in an attempt to inflate his gasping lungs, fought hard to maintain his arrogant facade.

Bloody hell!

For all that was holy. He considered rushing into the chapel, dropping to his knees and giving thanks. Indeed, it took a tremendous amount of effort not to look to the heavens and give a knowing wink.

Madame Labelle was certainly no middle-aged hag. The woman could be no more than five-and-twenty.

There were no hideous moles or warts. Her pure porcelain skin needed no paints or powders. His gaze drifted up to her honey-gold hair. It hung loosely around her shoulders, and he imagined the ends were long enough to brush against the base of her spine. An image of her lying naked in his bed flashed into his mind. He cursed Dane for not warning him he would be giving sanctuary to the goddess Venus.

The woman ran a bawdy house he reminded himself, mentally shaking his head. Although looking at her plain, simple gown, she looked more like a vestal virgin. Oh, he had no doubt she could keep the sacred flame in his hearth alight.

Damn it. He couldn't just stand there staring. He had to say something.

"Madame Labelle. Let me welcome you."

She glanced at him briefly, not bothering to look at his unconventional choice of attire. As a woman skilled in the art of seduction and titillation, he expected a flirtatious comment or a suggestive wiggle of the hips. But he received neither.

"You are Mr. Danbury I presume?" she asked, raising her chin.

Her voice sounded too haughty, too lofty for his liking. She could stop with the pretence. He was not a randy lord seeking proof she ran a higher class establishment.

"I am," he replied, intrigued by the smile that touched her lips as she scanned the exterior of the ancient stone building.

"And this is a monastery?"

"It was a monastery, but now it is my home."

"Is there still a chapel?"

"A small one."

Why did she ask so many questions?

"Excellent," she beamed, her face alight with pleasure and he had to blink from being blinded by the sheer brilliance of it all.

Marcus shuffled uncomfortably on the spot.

Perhaps it would have been easier if she had been an old hag with a crude mouth and a saggy bosom. The thought forced him to focus on her petite frame. In stark contrast to her steely composure, she appeared delicate and fragile, and he guessed her small breasts would fit nicely into his warm palms.

Roused by a sudden suspicion that this was a trick concocted by Dane for his own amusement, Marcus chose to be rude. "You seem eager to visit the chapel. Have you come here to repent?"

"Perhaps." She eyed him suspiciously but showed no sign she had taken offence. "In any given situation, one must make the most of the opportunities presented before them."

Marcus considered her cryptic words. Was she referring to her scandalous past? Did she consider him an opportunity to line her pockets? By God, he'd be tempted to pay just to satisfy his curiosity.

He stepped closer. It had been years since he'd felt such a strong pulse of desire.

"Perhaps I should follow your philosophy and make the most of the opportunity standing before me," he said with a smirk. He decided it best to be blunt for he had no intention of playing her mind games. "It's been a while since I've bedded a woman as fetching as you or with half the skill when it comes to pleasing men."

The slap came quick, sharp, stinging his cheek, albeit temporarily.

Tristan gasped but then raised a brow to suggest Marcus deserved nothing less.

That did not stop his blood boiling and bubbling away inside, and he clenched his jaw for fear of growling.

Who the hell did she think she was? Perhaps the woman had forgotten she spent all of her working hours on her back.

"Let me make a few things clear, Mr. Danbury, before we proceed any further." Her blue eyes flashed a hard frosty stare. "My name is not Madame Labelle. That name was given to me, forced upon me and I have borne it for far too long. I do not know what Lord Danesfield has told you. But from your crude and presumptuous manner, I can only guess. You should know I have left that world behind me, too." She exhaled deeply, a tired, weary sound and a frisson of guilt coursed through him. "Now, let me thank you for your hospitality and for offering me a place to stay."

She held out her hand. He didn't know whether to kiss it, turn his back or drop to his knees and swear undying loyalty.

He took her bare hand, ignoring the sparks of desire flitting through him and brushed his lips against the soft skin. It took a tremendous effort not to linger over it as the sweet smell of almonds flooded his nostrils.

"Forgive me, if I caused any offence. If you no longer wish to be known as Madame Labelle, how would you prefer to be addressed?" He could not hide the note of contempt in his tone.

As she glanced up at Haines, the coachman offered a reassuring smile and nodded his head as though encouraging her to continue.

"My ... my given name is Anna." The words stumbled from her lips but then she repeated with a little more confidence, "My name is Miss Anna Sinclair."

CHAPTER 2

Anna Sinclair.

She repeated the words over and over again in her mind. Other than revealing the truth to Haines during their journey, she had not uttered that name in years.

The truth was written on the first page of the Bible she kept at her bedside. Though she never dared to open the leather-bound book and only found the courage to lay her hand on the cover in silent prayer.

Anna Sinclair was like a distant relative: someone whose blood flowed through her veins. Someone who shared a kinship, yet she never visited the girl she once knew. Separating the past and the present had been her way of coping, of preventing the poison tainting everything she held dear.

Marie Labelle was nothing more than her adopted name. The name thrust upon her when Lucifer called to claim her soul.

She glanced up at the facade of the ancient stone building. The Lord revealed himself in a series of signs, or so her father had once said. To send a woman, rotten and riddled with sin, to a monastery was enough to rouse a faint flicker of faith in the hardest heathens.

Mr. Danbury may have mocked her, but in truth, she would use her time here to repent.

Her gaze drifted to the gentleman whose crude assumptions revealed him to be shallow and uncouth. While she imagined some women found his rough appearance becoming, she had seen enough of men to know his failure to follow convention most probably stemmed from a deep-rooted resentment.

Not that she cared.

A strong jaw and muscular frame offered little to no appeal. She had come to see one gentleman's body much like another, the sight of which left her cold. In that respect, her time with Victor had been educational. It had taught her to value honesty, humility and kindness above beguiling eyes and a charming smile.

"I have a letter from Lord Danesfield, proof he sent me here," she said.

"You're in the company of Haines. That's proof enough. But you may leave it on the desk in the chapter house."

"The chapter house?"

"I shall give you a brief tour and then show you to your room, Miss Sinclair." Mr. Danbury's tone sounded a little less arrogant. However, the air around them whirled with tension and hostility. "After such a long journey, I'm sure you'll want to wash and change your clothes."

"I'm afraid I left in rather a hurry and only brought a few items with me." Miss Beaufort had helped her pack a small bag, but Anna had not been of sound enough mind to care. "Is there somewhere locally where I may purchase what I need?"

Mr. Danbury gave a curt nod. "I'm sure Tristan will escort you to the village in the morning. He can act as translator—"

"I speak the language fluently, Mr. Danbury."

The gentleman's curious gaze drifted over her.

"I would be happy to escort you wherever you wish to go," Tristan replied.

Anna listened for the ugly sound of lust hidden beneath his words. Years of deceit and degradation made one doubt the smallest of thoughtful gestures. But she heard only sincerity, an eagerness to be helpful and friendly.

"Thank you, Mr. …"

"Mr. Wells," he replied, offering a bow one would give to a lady. "But I insist you call me Tristan. There's no need for formality, at least not here."

Anna gave a weak smile before scanning Mr. Danbury's bristled jaw and crumpled shirt. Compared to his friend, he looked like the destitute relative. "I can collect anything you may need whilst there Mr. Danbury. A comb, shaving implements, a clean shirt perhaps?"

Tristan sniggered and then pursed his lips.

"That won't be necessary." Mr. Danbury gestured to her bare hands. "But I should see what they have for chapped skin. You'll be expected to earn your keep whilst here."

Panic flared. There was only one way a man expected a whore to earn her keep.

"You will be expected to perform certain household chores," Mr. Danbury added as though party to her thoughts. "I trust that will not be a problem."

Relief coursed through her. "I am perfectly capable of cooking and cleaning," she replied only too eager to keep herself busy. "If you provide me with a list of duties, I will be more than happy to contribute. However, I do ask for an hour each day, where I may do whatever I choose."

Mr. Danbury offered a curt nod and charged off through the open doorway, no doubt expecting her to follow.

Tristan waved his hand towards the arched entrance. "Dare you risk entering the lion's lair?" he mocked, his face brimming with amusement. "Take it from me, his roar is far worse than his bite, his tone sharper than his teeth."

Anna stared thoughtfully at the door. "Mr. Danbury is a

playful kitten compared to what I am used to."

"Forgive me." Tristan cleared his throat. "I did not mean to be insensitive to your situation."

"You should also know that nothing you could say or do would offend me, Mr. Wells."

There was a brief moment of silence while he studied her.

"I understand." He turned to face her fully. "I too have placed a wall of ice around my heart. It is easier to convince ourselves we feel nothing than to live in constant pain."

She was not prepared to address the honesty in his words, and so she did what she always did when faced with the truth. She feigned indifference.

"Do not presume to know me, Mr. Wells. I've often wondered if I have a heart."

A smile touched his lips, and she knew he could see through her disguise. "I insist you call me Tristan," he said, ignoring her comment. She found she had gained a modicum of respect for him, purely because he had no desire to force his point. "Now, I shall assist Haines in stabling the horses and will arrange for your luggage to be taken up to your room."

A wave of anxiety caused her to stiffen and her gaze shot to Haines, who gave her a reassuring nod. "I'll see as all your belongings are kept safe," Haines said. "You can trust in that."

The coachman knew what her Bible meant to her. She could hardly walk around the monastery hugging it to her chest. Mr. Danbury really would believe she had pious intentions.

She wondered what he would say if he knew he had agreed to give refuge to a murderer.

As though summoned by pure thought alone, the gentleman in question strode back out through the arched doorway and glared. "I do not have time to wait while you stand conversing. Follow me, Miss Sinclair."

"Forgive me," she said, suppressing her amusement. True anger revealed itself in the eyes. Victor's black beady stare was a look terrifying enough to send wolves scampering. Mr. Danbury's warm brown gaze told her all she needed to know. "I assumed you had gone to make yourself more presentable."

Mr. Danbury brushed his hands through his shoulder-length hair. "This is presentable. Not that it is any concern of yours. You'll find no fancy lords here, all trussed up in their finery, spouting babble."

Anna resisted the urge to clap her hands together. Compared to Victor, Mr. Danbury was easy to read when it came to his emotions. Resentment was the motivation for his comment. Had he failed to meet the high expectations of a certain woman, she wondered? Or did he feel a sense of inadequacy when it came to the aristocracy?

Time would tell.

"And for that I am grateful, Mr. Danbury." She had no desire to argue and feed his frustration. When it came to defusing volatile situations, no one was more skilled. "I've heard more than my fair share of burble from obnoxious nobles to make me want to race for the hills at the mere thought of it. Rest assured, I admire those with the integrity to adhere to their principles."

Mr. Danbury's mouth opened and then he snapped it shut. He did not know what to make of her—that much was obvious.

Who had ever heard of a whore preach of integrity?

Anna took a step forward and stopped. "Thank you, Mr. Wells, for the warm welcome. Haines, I hope to continue our philosophical discussions this evening." Wearing a wide grin, both men inclined their heads. She walked up to Mr. Danbury. "Once you have given your tour, I should like to spend an hour in the chapel, if I may?"

He swallowed visibly, drawing her gaze to the open neck of his shirt. "You may spend the rest of the day as you wish. Tomorrow, you will take up your duties like the rest of us."

"That is most generous." She offered him her brightest smile. His blunt manner had no effect on her countenance, and she wondered if he was still brooding from the sharp slap he had received. “Please, lead the way, Mr. Danbury.”

He escorted her through the nave, but the rows of pews were no more, and now the wide walkway acted as a passage to the rest of the building.

“There’s a small chapel at the end there, located in the north transept,” he said, pointing to the left as he marched on ahead. She followed him out through the cloisters and into the garth. “You may use this area for recreation. The well in the centre is functioning and the water’s safe to drink.”

Anna glanced around the neat garden. A narrow pathway in the shape of the cross split the grass into four equal segments. There were numerous benches dotted along the route and depending upon the time of day she supposed one had a choice of sitting in the sun or the shade.

“It’s very peaceful here,” she said, gazing up as the sun warmed her skin. A wave of contentment rippled through her as she inhaled the clean air. “I imagine this is a rather pleasant place to sit in quiet contemplation.”

“I’ve never spent that much time out here,” he replied, gazing up at the cloudless sky as though only noticing its beauty for the first time.

“I’m surprised. You strike me as a man who enjoys being out of doors.”

“Why?” he said with a smirk. “Did you make that assumption based on the scruffy nature of my dress?”

“No,” she remarked casually. “Your skin has a bronze glow to it. The faint lines at the corners of your eyes suggest time spent squinting from the sun.”

“What, so now I dress like a beggar and have the face of a man in his dotage. You are brimming with compliments, Miss Sinclair.”

He had the face of a pirate plundering the high seas: fearsome and determined with a courageous charm. "You have the face of a man who is not frightened to work for what he wants."

A smile touched the corners of his mouth, and he inclined his head. "Then I withdraw my objection and pay homage to your insight and skills of observation."

Ah, another little clue he had unwittingly revealed.

He was proud of his work and wanted others to recognise the achievement. Any ordinary man would not think it worth the mention. Mr. Danbury's lineage must surely embrace at least one member of the aristocracy. Perhaps he had an estranged relative who despised how he lived here.

"Having a keen observation has been key to my survival," she replied, dismissing the grotesque vision of Victor filling her head. Whilst at the monastery she should try to stop being so suspicious of people's motives. She should not be so quick to strip back each word or comment.

She should not be so quick to judge.

Aware of Mr. Danbury's curious gaze, she wandered over to the well and peered inside. A ray of light reflected off the water far below. "Hello!" The word echoed and she couldn't help but chuckle. It had been a long time since she'd been free enough to express such a simple thing as joy.

"One of the servants will assist you should you need to draw water," Mr. Danbury said as though she lacked the skill necessary to lift a bucket.

Anna swung around to face him. He was standing with his arms folded across his chest. "We had a well in the village at home," she said calmly. "Once, I overheard someone say that a highway robber had hidden his loot at the bottom before racing off across the green. It was just a tale, but I would often raise the bucket in the hope of finding treasure."

"You grew up in the country?" He seemed surprised.

"I did," she replied, but had no intention of revealing anything more. "Shall we continue with the tour?"

He nodded and strode off along the path.

"We eat in the refectory," he said, leading her into a room long enough to seat a hundred men. "There is no formality when it comes to dining. Sometimes the servants sit with us. Sometimes I eat in the chapter house. You may do whatever you please."

Anna sighed. "Whatever I please or whatever pleases me?"

He gave an impatient wave. "Are they not the same?"

"No. But never mind."

They continued in silence. After a brief glance at the parlour, the *reredorter*: a room for washing and seeing to one's *toilette,* they continued to the upper floor.

"There are no fireplaces up here, and it can get cold at night. I've converted the old dormitory into small rooms. It helps minimise the draughts." He stopped outside an oak door, one of a handful situated along the corridor, his hand gripping the handle. "You may use this room for the duration of your stay. It is basic but should be adequate for your needs."

Anna waited for him to open the door but he seemed hesitant.

"Are we to go inside?"

"Of course." He shook his head, opened the door and gestured for her to enter

Anna felt a sudden flutter in her chest at the wonderful sight before her. The exposed stone of the exterior wall had a golden hue. Accompanied by the pale yellow drapes, the room felt warm and welcoming. The wrought-iron bed called out to her aching limbs, and she couldn't wait to snuggle into it and let the strain of the last few days melt away.

"I'm afraid there's no mirror—"

"I won't need one," she interjected.

"There are more blankets in the chest if you're cold and the brazier at the end of the hall can be brought in if needed. However, I ask you not to fall asleep whilst it's lit."

As a girl, she would have thrown her arms around him to express her gratitude. As a woman with a hardened heart, she merely smiled.

"Thank you, Mr. Danbury. The room is more than adequate." She noticed the candlestick on the side table. In London, it would be dawn before she crawled into bed. Here, she would have to find something to occupy her mind at night. "Would you happen to have any books I may borrow?"

He narrowed his gaze. "You are free to look over my personal library and take anything that interests you. Come down to the chapter house when you've settled in. As you leave the chapel, it is the first room on the left."

"I feel I must thank you again for your hospitality."

He made no comment. It occurred to her that perhaps he'd had little choice in the matter. Either way, she appreciated his generosity and offered a smile as he inclined his head and left the room.

Anna closed the door behind him and pressed her back to it as she surveyed the chamber. It had been years since she'd had a good night's sleep. There would be no constant banging above stairs. No piggish grunts of satisfaction echoing along the hallway. No gut-wrenching pain at the thought Victor might come home.

It suddenly hit her again. Victor was dead.

No matter where she ate or slept, no matter how hard she tried to forge a new life, she would always have his blood on her hands.

The memory of his last gasp for breath would haunt her forever.

CHAPTER 3

Marcus sat back in the chair, propped his feet up on his desk and perused the sealed letter in his hand. He recognised the elegant script and the circular heraldic mark pressed into the wax. Miss Sinclair had been his guest for a little over a week; this was the second letter to arrive for her from Dane.

Curiosity burned away.

Did the marquess want the woman for his mistress? Haines had made no secret of his master's fondness for a lady named Sophie Beaufort. Perhaps he wanted to wed one and bed the other. So, why would Dane ship Miss Sinclair off to France and then bombard her with letters? It made no sense.

For a man adept at discovering information, Marcus still knew nothing more of Miss Anna Sinclair, other than what she'd told him on her arrival. The woman did her utmost to avoid him, which suited him well. Such a ravishing beauty would tempt any man, and she had a beguiling charm he felt drawn to. Knowing she was vastly experienced in the bedchamber did not help matters. Whenever she moistened her lips or arched her back to relieve her aching muscles, his rampant mind conjured all sorts of lewd images.

His attention drifted up to the clock on the mantel as it struck one.

Miss Sinclair would be sitting out in the garth as she always finished her chores by twelve. Indeed, the woman was so regimental in her routine he knew exactly where to find her no matter what the time of day.

Dragging his feet off his desk, he jumped up and strode out of the door, hovering behind a pillar in the cloisters as he decided not to reveal himself immediately.

As predicted, Miss Sinclair was sitting on the bench, the bright rays of the sun casting a shimmering glow over her honey-gold hair. Damn. He felt the same deep stirring he always felt upon seeing her and he resisted the urge to stamp his foot until the dull thud shook the tiled walkway.

In a fit of frustration, he stomped out into the garth and cleared his throat to draw her gaze from a nondescript point of interest on the grass.

"You have another letter," he said, clutching the item in his hand, aware that his chest felt unusually tight, that his heart gave an odd flutter when her vivacious blue eyes met his.

"Good afternoon, Mr. Danbury." Her gaze drifted over his open shirt, up to the hair he had tied back in a queue and she offered him an angelic smile. "Isn't it a beautiful day?"

He glanced up, yet found nothing particularly enchanting, other than the woman sitting on his bench. "I had not noticed," he replied honestly. "I have been indoors for most of the morning."

Miss Sinclair tapped the empty seat next to her. "Then won't you sit for a moment."

Marcus stared at the hand resting on the wooden slats. A week ago, it had been smooth, soft and creamy, the nails clean and shaped. They had been the sort of hands a man longed to feel caress the tired muscles in his shoulders, trace circles in the fine hair on his chest. Now, chapped, red and raw at the knuckles, the nails short and misshapen, they were the hands of a woman from the workhouse.

Guilt flared.

Swallowing his apprehension, he slid into the seat next to her as though his weight would trigger the slats to snap and he would fall into a pit of spitting vipers.

She held out her rough hand, and he stared at it.

"The letter, Mr. Danbury. You said I had a letter."

Marcus shook his head and handed her the folded paper. "Do you not have anything to help soothe the sore skin on your hands?"

She examined the seal and sighed before splitting the red wax in two. "No. I must remember to buy a balm or a salve when I next go down to the village."

"If you speak to Selene in the kitchen, she may have something here that will help. She is quite knowledgeable when it comes to herbs and potions."

The corners of her mouth curled up into a grateful smile, and then she turned and focused her attention on the missive.

"Shall I leave you to read in private?" he asked.

"No." The word sounded like a soft sigh. "I'm done." She refolded the paper and placed it in her lap.

Desperation gripped him, an urge to know what the hell Dane wanted with her. Why had he written to her twice in the space of a few days?

"If you leave your reply on my desk in the chapter house, I shall send it along with my own correspondence in the morning."

"There is no need. I shall not be sending a reply."

Putting pressure on the quill was sure to sting her cracked knuckles. "If your hands pain you, Tristan can be trusted to write while you dictate."

Her penetrating gaze searched his face. Why did he get the impression she had the power to see beyond his words? The thought was somewhat unnerving.

"Are you telling me you cannot be trusted, Mr. Danbury?"

Marcus shrugged. "I know how fond you are of Tristan. I assumed you would prefer to spend time in his company rather than mine."

He had no desire to sit with her conversing of poets, the hidden meanings behind paintings, and her interest in gothic novels. He would use his time more wisely. Were her lips as soft and as sweet as he imagined? Would her skill and experience coupled with her beguiling beauty make for a more stimulating encounter in the bedchamber?

"I do not wish to reply because I have nothing to say," she said, although she offered no objection to his assessment of her friendship with Tristan.

A faint sliver of jealousy crept through him.

Bloody hell.

He cared for Tristan like a brother. He was the closest thing he had to family, yet the thought of punching him on the nose and marring his fine features suddenly had some appeal.

"Here, you may read it if you wish." She offered him the letter, but he waved his hand to decline.

"I have no interest in the details contained in your private correspondence, Miss Sinclair." The lie fell easily from his lips.

"It is from Lord Danesfield. He makes certain demands, and I refuse to comply."

Damn the woman. She knew exactly how to pique his interest. If he did ever pursue a liaison with her, he was certain she would have him pining after her like a lost puppy.

Unable to resist, and telling himself he had every right to know of any demands made upon his guests, he peeled back the folds and scanned the letter with feigned indifference.

Dane's extreme anger and frustration were evident within the first few lines. As he continued reading, Marcus felt a strange sense of relief when he realised Dane had no interest in having Miss Sinclair as his mistress.

How odd that the thought should please him.

Marcus glanced up into turquoise-blue eyes tinged with guilt. "Dane wants you to tell him what you know of Miss Beaufort's disappearance. Am I right to assume his previous letter was of a similar vein?"

Miss Sinclair nodded. "Lord Danesfield is a good man. To some extent I owe him my life. But I cannot tell him what he wants to know."

"You can't tell him, or you won't tell him?"

She shrugged. "Perhaps both are true. It doesn't matter now. It is not my secret to tell."

Marcus glanced down at Dane's scrawling script. Besides anger, the words held a hint of desperation. "But you do know Miss Beaufort is safe and well?"

"Of course she is safe and well. But Miss Beaufort knows her own mind. She is in love with him but fears she would not be a suitable wife for a marquess. She needs to know he loves her for who she is. When he talks of marriage, she needs to know it is not simply because Society dictates they should wed."

Dane was a man of strong principles. A man who would stop at nothing to protect those he cared for. If he had discussed marriage with Miss Beaufort, Marcus was damn sure he meant it. What Society deemed appropriate would play no part in his decision.

"Did Lord Danesfield send you here as a form of punishment? Are you to stay until you confess? Is that why you spend an hour each day in the chapel?"

The questions were impertinent, far too intrusive.

"Trust me, Mr. Danbury. Lord Danesfield could tie me to the rack and threaten to gouge my eyes and still it would not be my secret to tell."

Marcus admired her integrity. Most women of his acquaintance could no sooner hold their water as hold their tongue. What a shame Miss Sinclair had not chosen a different profession. With her beauty and unshakable resolve, she should be spying for the Crown.

"Dane is not the sort of man to give up. Don't be surprised to see him riding across the bridge on his stallion, smoke billowing from its hooves, its master's eyes as dark as night."

Miss Sinclair shivered visibly.

"I did not mean to frighten you," Marcus continued, dismissing the urge to wrap his arms around her and offer comfort. "I know how determined Dane can be."

"I do not fear Lord Danesfield," she said, glancing down to her lap. When she looked up at him, the pain in her eyes was unmistakable. "But I've felt the Devil's cold black stare. I know the difference between empty threats and the cruel, wicked intentions of a man with no conscience."

A man aroused and in his cups could certainly be a formidable opponent for any woman on her own. But he sensed her experience amounted to more than the hazards one encountered when running a brothel.

"Pay no heed to my strange ramblings," she continued before he could find the right words to ease her pain. "The streets of Marylebone can be treacherous at night."

"Most places are unsafe at night, Miss Sinclair." Indeed, even the coastal villages of northern France had their share of criminal activity. He should know. His nightly patrols had uncovered a violation of the law; now he had a duty to intervene.

She gave a weak smile. "You're right. It is best not to dwell on such things." She took the letter from her lap and stood. "I should return to my chores," she said, and he knew that at two o'clock she spent an hour in the chapel. At three, she spent an hour helping Selene prepare dinner.

"Of course," he stood, too, and offered a curt nod.

"Would you mind doing something for me, Mr. Danbury?" Her soft melodic tone held a trace of gratitude, and he doubted he could refuse her request.

"That depends on what it is you're asking," he said in an attempt to sound indifferent.

"Would you write to Lord Danesfield on my behalf? Would you ask if he knows what has happened to my girls?"

Had she used her womanly wiles to tempt him: stroked her hair, let the tip of her tongue trace the line of her lips, moved closer, so the scent of almonds made him want to taste her skin, he would have refused. But her request conveyed a level of trust in his ability to do the honourable thing and it touched him.

"Your girls?" he said. "Do you mean the women who work for you?"

"They no longer work for me, Mr. Danbury. To some extent they never did. I was simply there to care for them. A mother. A bank clerk. A modiste."

He raised his chin in acknowledgement. "What of his request for information regarding Miss Beaufort's whereabouts?"

Miss Sinclair appeared to contemplate his question.

"Tell Lord Danesfield that Miss Beaufort is safe and well."

Marcus shrugged. "That is all?"

"That is all," she nodded.

He inclined his head, and they walked until under cover of the cloisters.

"Thank you for your company, Mr. Danbury," she said as she turned away from him and headed towards the chapel.

Marcus watched her until she disappeared from view. He had never met a woman like Miss Sinclair. She was certainly not like the scantily clad bawds one found lounging about in brothels. More's the pity. The idea of her soft curves draped in diaphanous silk made his mouth water.

Now he came to think of it, she was not like any other woman he had ever met. In his experience, women fell into specific categories: self-absorbed, simpering, or slow-witted. So far, he'd found his guest to be thoughtful, intelligent, kind yet steely. She had the face of an angel, the body of a goddess.

How in God's name had she ended up running a house of ill repute?

More importantly, why had Dane sent her to France?

What was she running away from?

The following day another letter arrived.

Marcus glared at Tristan from the chair behind his desk. "I swear if this is from Dane I shall travel to London myself and ask him what the hell is going on."

"The gentleman does seem rather persistent." Tristan sniggered as he lounged back in the chair. "He hasn't even given her a chance to reply. But you know Dane."

Marcus flipped it over and did not know whether to sigh with relief or frustration when he recognised Dudley Spencer's initials pressed into the wax.

"Our friend is so desperate to find his love he has roped Dudley in to do his bidding."

"Would you like me to take the missive and find Anna?" Tristan asked, pushing his golden locks from his brow.

It grated that Tristan and Miss Sinclair were on such friendly terms that they had agreed to use their given names. In his home, there was no need to follow convention and the nature of Miss Sinclair's profession deemed any such fears void. Still, Marcus found it highly irritating.

"There's no need," Marcus said, suppressing his annoyance. "The letter is addressed to me."

Marcus placed the sealed missive back on his desk. He would deal with it later when his mood had improved. Now, another thought occupied his mind.

"Can I ask you something?"

Tristan raised a brow and nodded. "Of course. I'm surprised you've not come straight out with whatever it is."

Marcus swallowed to clear the uncomfortable lump in his throat. "It's about Miss Sinclair. I wondered if you have developed a fondness for her. A fondness that amounts to more than a shared interest in paintings and books."

Tristan shook his head, a glimmer of disappointment flickering in his blue eyes. "In all the years you've known me, you need to ask?"

Marcus couldn't quite fathom why he felt an overwhelming need to pry and gave an indolent wave to hide his slight embarrassment. "I thought spending time in the company of a beautiful, intelligent woman might make a difference."

Tristan snorted. "While Anna is all that you say, I still find it hard to imagine her working in a brothel, there will only ever be one woman for me."

Marcus could not comprehend his friend's mentality. The woman Tristan loved was married to another. Why could he not move on with his life?

"It's been five years, Tristan."

"I don't care if it's been fifty years. My feelings for Isabella will never change." Tristan exhaled deeply and shook his head. "But you've obviously developed a respect for Anna whilst she's been here. Do you not have an interest in her yourself?"

Marcus gave a contemptuous chuckle. "I will not tread in the footsteps of London's dissolute peers. Despite Miss Sinclair's appeal, I refuse to behave like the hypocritical lords of the *ton*."

"You refuse to behave like your father, you mean."

Marcus shrugged, but the mere mention of his father caused bile to bubble in his throat.

"I believe you would enjoy her company," Tristan continued, "if only you'd drop your guard. Although the seductive skills you usually employ to glean information from women would be lost on her. She is far too observant, not easily wooed."

"I have no intention of wooing her. I regard Miss Sinclair as just another assignment." Well, that's what he told himself when lying in his bed at night.

"Just another assignment?" Tristan yelled. "God, Marcus, sometimes you sound like a hard-hearted prig."

Marcus grabbed Dudley's letter. "We're to take care of her until Dane says otherwise. That's to be the extent of our involvement." God, he really did sound cold-hearted. "Besides, we have an obligation to focus on our current assignment."

Tristan shuffled forward. "Are we to go out again tonight?"

"We must go out every night until we find what we're looking for."

Tristan glanced at the mantel clock and then stood abruptly. "Then there are a few things I must attend to first."

"Don't tell me you're going to catch a few hours' sleep?" Marcus jested.

Tristan's face flushed. "You know I struggle to stay awake late. I'll not function properly if I'm tired."

"Good God, man. You were fine when we were forced to stay awake for three days to watch the gaol."

"Yes, but it's as though it triggered something inside. I'll just need a couple of hours."

"Go then," Marcus waved him away and offered a wide grin. "Go take your nap."

As soon as Tristan left the room, Marcus tore open the letter in his hand.

He was correct in his assumption. Dudley was determined to act on their friend's behalf and had specifically requested Marcus' help in persuading their guest to reveal all she knew of Miss Beaufort's whereabouts.

Bloody hell.

Marcus resisted the urge to kick the desk.

What did he have to do to repay the debt he owed to Dane? Sell his soul to the Devil by the sound of it.

It appeared Miss Sinclair truly was to be one of his assignments.

But how the hell would he get her to confess?

CHAPTER 4

Anna stood at her bedchamber window and watched the two riders cross the bridge on their way down towards the gate. For the third night in a row, Tristan and Mr. Danbury had left the monastery on some mysterious escapade, and they would not return until the early hours.

Where on earth were they going?

The first night, she imagined they were off to the local inn. Two strong, virile men would no doubt be seeking female companionship. Perhaps they had mistresses down in the village or enjoyed the company of tavern wenches. While she could imagine Tristan drinking ale and sharing friendly banter with the villagers, Mr. Danbury appeared far too serious to partake in rowdy games and bouts of playful teasing.

Indeed, his solemn disposition suggested one of two things. The gentleman's mind was overwhelmed with a matter of grave importance, or his mood was marked by a deep sense of anguish.

Perhaps both were true.

Either way, he appeared to be a man of strong, brooding passions. One did not have to stand close to know a fire burned brightly inside, simmering hot just beneath the surface. It would not take much for him to lose his temper and she wondered when he loved if he did so with the same heated fervour.

Not that it mattered to her.

She would never trust another man again.

How could she when memories of Victor lingered in the dark places of her mind?

Pushing all thoughts of Victor aside, she focused on the mystery of Mr. Danbury's last night departures. After stumbling upon a private meeting earlier in the day, she now knew it had nothing to do with seeking an amorous liaison. The raised voices echoing from inside the chapter house revealed a disagreement over the best way to proceed with their assignment.

Assignment?

The word had been clear, specific, but the nature of their enquiry remained a mystery.

Mr. Danbury acted with a certain apprehension in her presence, although he was far more hospitable since their conversation in the garth. She often found him looking in her direction when he thought she wouldn't notice. Her overly suspicious mind played its cunning tricks and refused to be tempered.

Anna convinced herself it all had something to do with Victor's death. It was too much of a coincidence—her arrival, their sudden, secret assignment.

What if Victor did have a contact abroad?

She knew he shipped girls out of London but had no idea where. He had kept it from her until the River Police had stepped up their patrols and he had been forced to hide a girl at Labelles.

What if his contact had followed her? What if he was here in France and knew she was the one responsible for killing Victor?

Had Lord Danesfield uncovered information and asked Mr. Danbury to investigate? They were situated on the coast after all.

The years she'd spent running Victor's establishment, were years spent in ignorance. She could never quite gauge his mood, never really knew what bizarre request would fall from his grim lips. She never knew the full extent of the dastardly deeds committed at his behest, and she'd be damned before she'd let another man play her for a naive fool.

Gathering the thick blanket and the candlestick from on top of the dresser, Anna made her way downstairs. The door to the chapter house was unlocked. She let herself in, placed her candle on the side table and settled into the wingback chair tucked away in the far corner of the room.

Despite the simplicity of the small vaulted chamber, it held an inherently masculine feel. The solid mahogany desk sat strong and proud in the middle of the room. The tiled floor and stone walls should have made it feel cold, but the leather-bound books lining the shelves on one wall created a blanket of rich autumnal colour. The moonlight beyond the solitary stained glass window brought the coloured image to life. The red hues of the saint's cloak coupled with the golden halo, creating its own sense of warmth.

If the last few nights were any indication, she would be waiting hours for their return. Pulling the blanket up around her shoulders, she shuffled further back into the seat and made herself more comfortable.

For the first fifteen minutes, she imagined numerous conversations with Mr. Danbury. Like a Covent Garden actress learning her lines, she used various tones and different mannerisms to convey the point that she insisted on knowing the nature of this secret assignment. If they were acting on her behalf, she deserved to know the truth.

As her lids grew heavy, she blinked and tried to fight the overwhelming need to sleep. Anna soon lost the battle of wills, her world descending into darkness as she closed her eyes.

"Good Lord, are you not going to bed?"

Tristan's voice permeated the peaceful realms of her mind.

"In a moment, there's something I need to do first."

Somewhere in the distance, she heard Mr. Danbury's reply,

heard the creaking of a door, the dull thud of boots on the tiled floor.

Anna's lids fluttered as she became accustomed to her surroundings and she saw the broad figure of Mr. Danbury standing before his desk. He had his back to her as he rummaged through his private papers. Even if she had not heard the patter of raindrops against the window, she knew from the damp ends of the wavy locks brushing his shoulders that the storm had broken.

Should she offer a discreet cough? Or should she wait for him to turn and notice her? The longer she sat there, the harder the decision became.

Mr. Danbury flicked the lid on the inkwell, dipped his pen and scratched a few notes. Once satisfied with his work, he sprinkled dust from the pounce pot over the wet ink, blowing away the residue.

She was about to speak when he tugged his shirt from his breeches and pulled it up over his head. He screwed it into a ball and wiped across his neck and shoulders. It was not the sight of his muscled torso that caused the odd flutter in her chest. Three raised rivulets ran across his back. The dark pink scars were thin, like the marks left from a beating with a strap or whip.

A faint gasp escaped from her lips.

He froze.

She knew he would turn around. She knew she had to find a way to remain calm and in control, to not be weak or easily overpowered.

"Mr. Danbury," she said, wrapping her blanket around her shoulders as she stood to greet him. "You're home at long last."

He drew in a deep breath before turning to face her. She expected anger, a sign of irritation at the very least. But the look she received from him caused the strange flutter to return.

"Miss Sinclair. Is everything all right?" His tone carried a hint of concern. "Are you ill? Has something happened?"

"No, no, nothing has happened." Why did she feel like a silly girl? If anything, his scars should have made him appear more vulnerable. But they only added to the air of mystery, enhanced the masculine appeal that captured her interest. "I have watched you ride out these past few nights, and I wanted to discuss it with you."

His suspicious gaze drifted over her and he stepped forward. Still clutching his shirt in his hand, he took the corners of her blanket and peeled them back as though expecting to find a wonderful gift hidden inside.

"You're still dressed," he said, the corners of his mouth curling down in disappointment. "Have you been waiting here for me all night?"

His seductive purr reminded her that men often have salacious thoughts at the mere turn of an ankle. Due to the nature of her profession, had he made the usual assumption? Did he imagine she sought him out with more licentious thoughts in mind?

With a sudden surge of anger, she snatched back her blanket. "What did you expect to find? Did you think to see me lounging on your desk wearing nothing more than long stays and white stockings? Should I rouge my lips a blood red? Should I pull grapes from a bunch using only my mouth?"

Mr. Danbury raised a sinful brow. "I cannot deny the thought has appeal." When she gave him a furious glare, he added, "I am joking. I merely meant you must have been waiting rather a long time."

"Oh. I thought you meant …"

"What?"

"Nothing."

Now she felt foolish again.

Her gaze drifted to the bronze skin and defined contours on his chest. Most gentlemen gracing the rooms of Labelles were pasty-white, an obvious paunch indicating their wealth and status. Mr. Danbury's muscled physique supported her comment that he was a man willing to work if need be. Standing in such proximity she felt a warm heat radiate from his skin, and she wondered if all men possessed a similar quality. Indeed, her personal experience lacked such intimate knowledge, as Victor had been the only man she'd ever been close to.

"Don't look so downcast," Mr. Danbury said with a hint of arrogance. "Now what was it you wanted to discuss?"

Anna couldn't think while he was standing there half naked. "Would you mind putting on your shirt? I think I prefer the peasant to the golden-skinned Lothario."

He chuckled. "I assumed you would be comfortable in the presence of a naked man. You must have seen more than your share."

Anna felt her face flush. "Must I slap you again, Mr. Danbury, in the hope you will learn to hold your foolish tongue." He really did let himself down when making such childish remarks.

His heated gaze penetrated her steely composure. When he stepped closer, she wasn't sure if he was about to unleash the wrath of the Devil or pull her into an embrace and plunder her mouth like the savage pirate his unconventional dress implied.

Both thoughts were unnerving. But, after what felt like a lifetime of cowering in the corner, she refused to relinquish control.

"You cannot intimidate me," she continued, raising her chin in defiance.

With a gleam in his eye, Mr. Danbury smiled as his gaze drifted to her lips. "And why would I want to do that, Miss Sinclair?"

"Because you like to dominate everyone and everything. Because you despise appearing weak and vulnerable."

He smirked at her honest appraisal. "That's where you're wrong. You err when you compare me to most men of your acquaintance. I am happy to admit I am weak." He inhaled deeply as his gaze travelled over her face and hair. "I am happy to admit that in your company I am vulnerable. You need only say the word, and I would yield to the power of your intelligence and beauty."

A strong masculine force penetrated the air around them. It was not the threatening or fearful sensation she was used to, and she was shocked to feel a tiny frisson of desire spark in her ice-cold body.

Believing herself immune to such feelings, it shook her to her core.

Anna Sinclair really was naive and foolish. Marie Labelle would think her pathetic for responding so easily to any man's fake protestations. Yet she could not shake the thought that there was a grain of truth hidden within his words.

"Flowery overtures often hide the worst of lies," she said, her tone bitter in a bid to reinforce the iron vault safeguarding her heart. Marie would be proud.

"You may call me what you will, but never call me a liar."

His words were blunt but lacked the poisonous venom that usually paralysed her with fear. Victor would have grabbed her chin or squashed her cheeks together with his long bony fingers. It seemed Mr. Danbury possessed at least one quality of a true gentleman.

"Forgive me," she said. "Perhaps I am too used to the cunning devices employed by a skilled seducer."

There was no mistaking her veiled insult and Mr. Danbury jerked his head in response. He stepped back. The distance brought with it the familiar coldness that shrouded her wherever she went.

"The hour is late or early depending how one looks at it," he said with indifference. He shook out his shirt and threw it over his head, thrusting his arms violently into the sleeves as though they had wronged him in some way. "You should retire to your chamber."

Anna swallowed deeply. "But you have not answered my question."

"I did not realise you had asked one."

"You have an assignment," she said, finding the courage to broach the subject as she would not rest until she knew the truth. "I heard as much earlier while you were arguing with Tristan."

"We were not arguing." Mr. Danbury perched on the edge of his desk and folded his arms across his chest. "What else did you hear?"

"Nothing." She shrugged. Everything else had sounded like incoherent mumbles. "But you rode out again this evening."

"What of it?"

"Well, it cannot be a coincidence. Lord Danesfield must have uncovered new information relating to the Comte de Dampierre." Just saying his name aloud caused the fine hairs at her nape to stand on end. Her stomach felt hollow; her heart wormed its way up into her throat. "Have you found his accomplice? Is he here, in France? Tell me, Mr. Danbury. You cannot hide it from me. I deserve to know the truth."

He stared at her and narrowed his gaze. "Dane mentioned your association with a Frenchman. This comte you speak of, is he your lover?"

"No," she cried. Heavens, the thought caused her to shudder. "He was many things but never that."

"He is your partner in business, then?"

"Dampierre shared nothing. He owned me, Mr. Danbury. I did his bidding, took care of his girls."

"He owned you, or he owned Labelles?"

Anna shrugged. "Both." She had come to find answers not be barraged with a multitude of questions.

"And now you have fled London with little more than the clothes on your back," he muttered to himself. "Did Lord Danesfield assist in your escape?"

Anna nodded. "He escorted me to the coast and saw me safely out of England."

Mr. Danbury jumped off the desk. "Bloody hell. Does Dane take me for a complete fool?" He paced the floor. "Did he not think to inform me that this Dampierre fellow could come looking for you?"

Anna grabbed the sleeve of his shirt and forced him to stop. "The comte will not come looking for me," she implored, hoping it would be enough to placate him. "I can promise you that."

"Revenge feeds the hearts of some men," he said with a hint of contempt as though she lacked his worldly experience in all matters. "Trust me. He will want justice for your betrayal. He will seek you—"

"Victor will not come looking for me," she repeated.

"A man who makes a living as he does will not be bested by a woman. You're his property. You probably know too much about his business dealings."

"He won't come." While she tried to sound confident, days of suppressed emotion pushed to the fore, and she could feel the tears welling. She had agreed never to mention the horrific events in the warehouse.

"How do you know? Damn it. I left you alone here tonight. How do you know he's not out there now waiting for you to wander down to the village on your own?"

A surge of raw emotion broke. "Because he's dead," she sobbed burying her head in her hands. Sucking in a breath, she looked up at him. "He won't come because I stabbed him in the back and watched him gulp his last breath. Because justice has already been served."

Mr. Danbury's eyes grew wide, and his mouth hung open as he shook his head. After what seemed like an hour, he placed his hands on her shoulders.

"You killed him?" he whispered, staring into her eyes as

though he had misheard. "Is that why Dane sent you here? So you wouldn't hang?"

She wiped away the tears streaming down her face. "Yes, and no. Lord Danesfield concocted a story to protect me. But you must understand I had no choice in the matter. Victor would have killed me."

"You should have told me," Mr. Danbury said as he pulled her into an embrace, rubbed her back as the tears continued to fall. "Dane should have trusted me with the information."

Anna let the warmth of his body surround her. For the first time in her life, she felt safe—if only for a moment. "I murdered him, Mr. Danbury, and all I can do now is repent."

CHAPTER 5

Marcus pulled Miss Sinclair closer to his chest, the smell of almonds flooding his nostrils as he whispered words of comfort into her hair. She felt soft and warm in his arms, and he fought the urge to claim her mouth, knowing that he would not be able to stop until he had claimed her body. Good Lord, why did she have to be so damn tempting? He could feel desire pulsing inside, feeding this strange craving he had for her.

Miss Sinclair had just confessed to murder. Emotions ran high. He could take advantage of her vulnerability. Once their lips met, she would be more than pleased with what he had to offer.

But even he wasn't that cold and callous.

Now he knew why she spent so much time in the chapel, praying, repenting, hoping the Lord would absolve her of her sins. Marcus understood the feeling. He had killed in self-defence, part of fulfilling his duty to the Crown. That didn't make it any easier, and he suspected the experience would haunt her forever.

So, Dane had sent her to France to protect her. The act of

chivalry told him all he needed to know. Had she not thrust the knife into the comte's back, someone else would have lost their life. Of course, Dane would also be protecting his own interests and Marcus knew there must surely be more to the story.

Guilt flared when he thought of Dudley Spencer's request for information.

"If it helps, you *can* talk to me," he said. His intention was not to pry, but merely to offer a means of easing her mental torment. "You should not keep your feelings hidden inside."

"Suppressing all emotion is the only way I know how to cope," she murmured against his chest.

"Guilt is like a disease." To his own mind, he sounded like a hypocrite. "It will fester and eat away at all the good until everything else is tainted, too."

He felt her shoulders rise as she took a deep breath. She stepped back and looked up at him, her eyes red and puffy. "I cannot recall the last time I cried, other than the night of Victor's death. But even then it felt different. I was numb to my emotions. There was, and still is, a large part of me that is not sorry."

"I understand." He pursed his lips and nodded. "For Dane to offer his protection, he must have felt the comte deserved his dreadful fate."

"Victor shot and killed a man right in front of us. It should have been me." She stared off into the distance, shook her head and muttered, "Poor Morgan. Victor would have killed us all in his desperation to flee with Miss Beaufort."

With every new snippet of information, Marcus was slowly piecing the story together.

"Miss Beaufort? The lady Lord Danesfield seeks?" Perhaps being in such a state of weakness, Miss Sinclair would change her mind and tell him where Dane's lady was hiding. "No wonder Dane is desperate to find her."

Miss Sinclair narrowed her gaze and shrugged. "Miss Beaufort is not in any danger. Lord Danesfield knows Victor is dead."

"Yes, but you mentioned an accomplice. You cannot blame Dane for fearing this person would seek revenge. You believed it to be so yourself. He must be worried for Miss Beaufort's safety."

Miss Sinclair seemed to ponder his words. "If there is an accomplice, he is not in England and he knows nothing of Miss Beaufort. I'm certain she is safe at the cottage."

"The cottage?"

Oh, this was going to be easier than he thought. Hopefully, he would not need to disclose information regarding Dudley's request. And that would sit easier on his conscience.

"Did I say cottage?" She cast him an arrogant grin. "How foolish of me."

The woman was shrewd. He preferred seeing a smile touching the corners of her mouth. Even though her face looked red and blotchy, her eyes appeared less sorrowful.

"So, Lord Danesfield told you nothing of Dampierre or his accomplice?" she continued.

Marcus shook his head. "Dane said nothing." But his friend would feel the sharp edge of his tongue for failing to explain the facts.

"And your nightly excursions have nothing to do with me?"

"No. Nothing." He was deliberately vague. The fewer people who knew of his assignment, the better. The men they were watching would not think twice about silencing a woman in the most brutal fashion.

"And you expect me to believe you?" she scoffed.

Marcus straightened. "I expect nothing. But after what you've just told me, under no circumstances are you to leave the monastery without my knowledge." It was wise to be cautious until Dane confirmed whether the comte's accomplice posed any real threat. "I want to know where you are at all times. Is that clear?"

He knew his tone sounded severe, but he was angry at Dane for his lapse of judgement. He was angry at Miss Sinclair for not informing him sooner. He was angry at himself for not being able to tell her she could trust him.

"I do not mean to frighten you," he added when he noticed her bottom lip tremble. "But in the years I've worked with Dane, I've discovered one can never be too careful."

"I have lived in a permanent state of fear for years, Mr. Danbury," she replied, squaring her shoulders and lifting her chin in a bid to regain her composure. "One more week will not be such a hardship."

One week? Knowing Dane's need for thoroughness and the severity of her situation, he planned to leave her in France for a month or two.

"And you will keep me informed of your movements?"

"I will," she reassured.

"At all times?"

"I will not leave the monastery without your permission."

There was no hint of sarcasm or resentment in her tone. She sounded grateful, appeared to be more relaxed in his company. Perhaps confessing her sins had helped her to lower her defences. Perhaps the intimate way he'd held her had forced him to lower his defences, too.

"Do you have any plans tomorrow?" he asked as he would need to organise his day around hers for the foreseeable future. "Will you be going to the fair? I hear there are to be jugglers and fire-eaters, music and dancing."

"Perhaps it may be best if I stay here."

He nodded. "Then I shall also stay behind. The sight of Tristan twirling around the maypole is enough to rouse nausea in a man with the strongest constitution."

She laughed. "Gentlemen don't twirl around the maypole.

Although with his poise and elegance, I am certain he would put all the maidens to shame. But I would not want you to miss the fair on my account."

Pushing through boisterous crowds, being hugged by those too inebriated to stand was not his idea of amusement. But after all she had been through, perhaps a few hours of mirth might lift her spirits.

"I would be happy to accompany you, should you change your mind," he said.

Happy was far from the appropriate term, but a show of benevolence would go some way to easing the guilt he felt. Dudley would continue to hound him until he'd discovered the secret of Miss Beaufort's whereabouts.

"You would not mind?" The glimmer of hope in her eyes felt like a punch in his deceitful gut.

"No. We could ride out in the afternoon, leave the fair before dusk." Before the drunken revellers became a nuisance. Besides, it would give him an opportunity to observe the men of the village, particularly the landlord of the inn, Lenard. Marcus suspected one of the locals was guilty of assisting in criminal activity.

"If you're sure. Even if we stay for an hour." Miss Sinclair smiled. He made a mental note to make her smile more often. The wonderful vision should not be hidden away like the best china, only to be brought out on rare occasions. "It's been years since I've had the freedom to enjoy such merry pursuits."

Oh, he could think of a whole host of merry pursuits that would keep her entertained for hours. Indeed, his manhood throbbed at the thought.

"I'm sure." He gave a curt nod. It was imperative he kept a close eye on her. And for his sake, he wanted to see her face alight with pleasure.

They stared at each other for a moment, not knowing quite what to say.

"I … I should escort you back to your chamber."

She shook her head. "That won't be necessary, Mr. Danbury. I will be safe enough inside these stone walls."

She was right. Besides, the thought of standing just a few feet away from her bed, from the place where she slid those soft thighs beneath the sheets, was far too tempting.

"Then I shall bid you goodnight, Miss Sinclair."

She smiled, and he felt truly blessed. "Goodnight, Mr. Danbury."

Marcus watched her leave the room, the gentle sway of her hips causing his body to flame. Sweet Jesus. To think she lay just a few doors away from him.

How the hell was he to survive a whole afternoon in her company?

But she was a madam of a brothel, he reminded himself.

And a damn enchanting one at that.

CHAPTER 6

Anna rushed to complete her chores by eleven. She wanted to use the extra hour to soak the dirt from beneath her fingernails, apply the balm to her knuckles, brush her hair and change into the only other dress she possessed. Gone were the days when she had to preen herself to perfection. Victor had always insisted she wore the clothes of a duchess.

"Behave like a whore and they will treat you like one," Victor had remarked, the contempt in his tone showing how much he despised the aristocracy. "Behave like a queen and all shall bow before you."

Anna glanced down at the plain muslin dress, lifting the hem to stare at the dusty leather half-boots. A snigger escaped as she imagined Victor's look of horror at such simple country attire. Wearing her cape and with her hair tied loosely at her nape, she would easily blend in with the folk from the village.

A knock on the door disturbed her reverie.

"Come in." She smiled when Selene entered her chamber carrying the tiny wooden pot. "Is that the balm you've made?"

Selene nodded. The woman spoke English although struggled when holding a lengthy conversation. "You must apply it every evening. It will sting but only for a few seconds." She reached into the pocket of her apron and removed two cotton squares. "Wrap these to your hands while you sleep."

Anna smiled. "*Merci*, Selene."

In the two weeks Anna had been at the monastery, she'd found Selene to be aloof, reserved. Perhaps she was shy or needed to concentrate on interpreting the language and so consequently appeared distant. When Anna had suggested they converse in French, she protested and said she needed to improve her English as Mr. Danbury often got frustrated with her when she failed to follow his instructions.

From what Anna had witnessed, Mr. Danbury was often frustrated with everyone.

"It's very kind of you to go to so much trouble," Anna continued, trying not to accentuate each word as if the woman were deaf. "Will you be going to the fair?"

"*Oui, madame,*" she nodded eagerly. "Yes, I am going with Andre."

Anna had no idea why she kept calling her *madame*. They were of a similar age after all. Although they were like night and day in terms of their colouring, even more so when it came to worldly experience. "Then I shall see you there. Mr. Danbury has kindly agreed to escort me a little later this afternoon."

Selene's brown eyes widened as her smile faded. "But Mr. Danbury, he never goes. He says he does not like the crowds."

Anna laughed in an attempt to lighten the mood as Selene appeared somewhat disturbed by the thought. "Perhaps that's because he is far too serious. It will do him good to drink ale and eat roasted pig while dancing with performing monkeys."

Selene gave a weak smile. "If you say so, *madame*."

"Don't worry about Mr. Danbury. We will only stay for a short while and ride back before dark."

Anna's words did not placate Selene, and although she nodded repeatedly, her eyes grew dark and distant.

"Thank you again for the balm," Anna said as the woman scurried out of the door without saying another word.

Pushing aside all thoughts of Selene's odd behaviour, Anna went to the chapel and spent an hour in quiet contemplation. The silence soothed her spirit. Still she received no further sign, no indication as to where fate's path would take her next.

The sound of booted steps echoing through the nave caught her attention, a sure sign her companion was ready to depart.

The gentleman in question cleared his throat. She did not have to turn around to know Mr. Danbury stood behind her. He walked with a heavier gait than Tristan and the air about her swirled with a strange tension: a sliver of apprehension mingled with excitement. The hairs on her nape tingled which never happened in the presence of any other man.

"Miss Sinclair." The deep timbre of his voice caused a weird shiver to race through her body, and she inhaled slowly and deeply in an attempt to maintain her composure.

"Mr. Danbury," she said, standing and turning to face him. Raising a brow in surprise at the sight of his cravat, she could not help but tease him. "Good heavens. Either someone has tried to strangle you with a piece of neckwear, or you have made an effort to smarten your appearance."

He gave an arrogant smirk in retaliation and tugged on the ends of his plain blue waistcoat. "At this precise moment, being strangled with a length of starched muslin has definite appeal."

She pursed her lips to suppress a smile as he craned his neck. "You do not need to wear it on my account. I am used to seeing you wander about as though you're ready to set sail and plunder the high seas."

"I shall take that as a compliment," he said, his eyes flashing with amusement. "A pirate has far more finesse than a peasant or beggar."

"By finesse, I assume you mean your skill and ability to deal with difficult situations." Indeed, there were not many men who would take a stranger into their home, give them food and lodgings despite discovering they had murdered the last gentleman who'd provided similar comforts.

He raised a confident brow. "By finesse, I speak of my consummate skill in most things, Miss Sinclair." He moistened his lips as his gaze drifted over her.

"Well, you certainly have a pirate's conceit and sense of superiority."

"There is nothing conceited about speaking the truth."

Anna folded her arms across her chest. "Then you must show me these marvellous skills of yours. Once at the fair, I'm sure there will be plenty of opportunities to demonstrate your extraordinary strength and agility."

"You mock me, but perhaps I may surprise you. But know I draw the line at wrestling with monkeys and bears."

She sniggered. Mr. Danbury could be very amusing when he wasn't stomping around growling at everyone. "Surely there will be jugglers and fire-eaters there. Let us see how you fare with them."

"I do have quite nimble fingers, and my body is already aflame." His velvety tone made her shiver, and she recognised the glaze of desire in his warm brown eyes. "I fear if I even attempt to eat fire I'll surely combust."

As Madame Labelle, she knew the feigned words of a seducer. As Anna Sinclair, she could not ignore the fluttering sensation in her stomach.

"What a shame the font is empty. A splash of holy water would surely help to douse the flames." She stepped forward. "Come. We shall be here trading quips until nightfall. If you're ready, I shall go and fetch my cape."

He inclined his head. "Give me a moment to find my cutlass and eyeglass and I'll meet you in the stable."

~

The fair was well under way by the time they rode down into the village. The boisterous laughter, the hawkers shouting their wares, and the singing and merry melody from the instruments of numerous minstrels permeated the air.

Anna scanned the vast sea of heads. They had no hope of spotting Tristan or Selene and Andre amongst the hordes of people packed into the field.

Mr. Danbury climbed down from his horse, paid the groom a *sou* and came round to help Anna down. She lowered the hood of her cape, and as his hands settled on her waist, she felt the strange frisson of awareness she always felt in his company.

"What would you like to do first?" he asked as he set her down. His large hands lingered there for a moment, and she felt the loss instantly when he stepped away.

"We could wander around. See what's here. I doubt we'll find Tristan."

He did not offer his arm, which suited her well enough. She was not used to being in the company of chivalrous men.

"Listen for the loudest laugh and we're guaranteed to find him," he snorted.

"I've never met anyone as cheerful as Tristan," she said as Mr. Danbury placed his hand at the small of her back to guide her through the crowd. Good Lord. The strange feeling came upon her again: a gurgling in her stomach, an erratic thumping in her chest. Hoping conversation would provide a distraction, she added, "Is he ever grumpy?"

Mr. Danbury pursed his lips as he pondered the question. "Only when he's tired. When I first met him, he rarely smiled. Anger was the only emotion he expressed."

Anna was shocked. "I can't imagine him wearing a permanent scowl. It would ruin his fine features."

"We all have our own way of dealing with pain," he replied, his tone a little strained, and she noted a hint of irritation. "Take you, for example. You choose solitude and quiet reflection as a way of coping. You are regimental in your routines, and can be found in the same place at the same time each day. Some would say it stems from a feeling of insecurity."

Anna glanced up at his solemn expression, surprised he had even bothered to notice her daily rituals. Being regimental about things did help her to feel calmer, more secure.

"Step closer." The hawker's cry disturbed her musing. "Step closer and watch his fingers work the willow."

The peddler stood in the middle of the path, guiding people to an area where a man sat weaving the pliant stems into baskets. They followed his direction, hanging back from the crowd as they had no real desire to witness the event.

Indeed, only one thought filled her head: Mr. Danbury had been watching her closely enough to form an accurate opinion of her character.

"How observant of you to notice something as mundane as my habitual activities," she said curiously.

"I notice everything, Miss Sinclair." His gaze wandered over her face, fell to the opening of her cape, scanned the outline of her breasts hidden beneath the unflattering muslin.

"And what of you?" she asked, swallowing deeply to stop her face from flushing. She had seen the bare behind of many a grunting lord, yet one suggestive glance and her cheeks flamed. "What odd mannerisms or traits reveal your preferred way of coping with pain?"

She knew the answer but wanted to hear it fall from his lips. Just thinking about how he may have suffered conjured an image of the scars marring the otherwise perfect skin on his back.

"I work."

The words were cold, blunt, yet clear. Judging by his muscular physique and sun-kissed complexion, he'd met with more than his fair share of distressing ordeals.

As they drifted away from the stall, she recalled the advice he'd given her over suppressing one's feelings and decided to use it against him.

"You can talk to me. It is not good or healthy to keep your feelings hidden."

A smile touched the corners of his mouth. "Who told you that?"

She laughed. "You did."

"Then I'm a fool masquerading as a great philosopher."

They paused on the path, and she pointed to the juggler demonstrating how easy it was to throw five apples into the air without dropping a single one.

"Or perhaps you are a great philosopher pretending to be a fool." She kept her eyes on the juggler but could feel Mr. Danbury's penetrating stare. "I believe your words reflect a certain wisdom. It is your grumpy countenance that makes you seem like a ninny."

"Grumpy?" he snorted. "Even a court jester would appear sullen when compared to Tristan."

"Now that's the fool talking again. It is not wise to compare yourself to others." She glanced at his cravat; the folds were less crisp and symmetrical than they ought to be. Even though he had tied his dark wavy hair back in a queue, he still bore the look of a rogue-come-pirate. "As a man who refuses to conform and dresses as he pleases, I expected you to know that."

"It was merely an observation," he said. "I have always had an air of discontent. I find, that way, one is never disappointed."

"And so that is how you deal with pain, besides working, of course. You make everyone believe you don't care."

"I find it more preferable than praying for salvation."

"Again, we all have our ways of coping." Anna breathed a sigh. "Now, I don't know about you, but I am tired of talking about feeling miserable and wretched. I suggest we find something to enliven our spirits."

"I have no objection." Mr. Danbury raised a sinful brow as he moistened his lips. "What did you have in mind?"

She could tell from his tone that his thoughts were licentious. In a bid to help ease his air of discontent, Anna decided, from now on, she would always be open and honest with him.

"Nothing amorous," she said, threading her arm through his and directing him along the path. "There are other ways to entertain oneself."

"Are there? I have yet to find anything as stimulating."

Oh, he had not lied. He did have a consummate skill for seduction. The smooth tone of his voice caused her breath to come a little quicker. The glint in his eye caused her heart to skip a beat.

"Then we must attempt to find something to satisfy you," she said as they passed a stall selling carved figures. "What about shaping wood? I'm sure it is an extremely relaxing pursuit."

"Possibly," he nodded, tucking her hand more securely into the crook of his arm. "I do enjoy running my hands over smooth surfaces."

Anna pursed her lips to prevent a chuckle from escaping. "What about composing songs or poetry based on myths and legends?" she said as they passed a minstrel singing a ballad.

"I'm certain I could make you sing a merry tune." His heated gaze penetrated her clothing, seeped into her skin to warm her blood. "I suppose I could compose a song detailing my valiance."

"And what courageous deed have you performed to boast of such things?"

"I have suffered a torturous trip to the fair just to please a maiden."

Anna did chuckle. "Perhaps you could add a verse about how you saved me from a terrible afternoon of chores."

For the first time since meeting him, his eyes glistened with genuine amusement and she found she rather liked seeing him so relaxed and carefree.

As though drawn to the sound of their laughter, she heard Tristan call out to them. She spotted him waving as he pushed through the crowd in a bid to reach them before they were lost in a bustling wave of eager revellers.

"Guess who won the archery contest?" Tristan's smile stretched so wide he flashed a full set of teeth.

"That's wonderful," she replied. "Isn't that wonderful, Mr. Danbury?"

"I doubt you had much competition," Mr. Danbury scoffed, although there was no hint of malice in his tone. "They should have blindfolded you to even the odds."

Tristan smiled. "I'll take that as a compliment."

"Have you seen Selene and Andre?" she asked. Hopefully, if Selene saw Mr. Danbury in a jovial mood, it might ease her fears.

"They were listening to the musicians when I last saw them." Tristan exhaled. "I'm going to head back as I need to catch a few hours' sleep. Are you coming?"

"In a little while," Mr. Danbury glanced at her. "But I won't need your company tonight. I'll be going out on my own."

Tristan's eyes widened as his gaze shot to Anna. She felt her heart race at the thought of Mr. Danbury riding alone in the dark. Heaven only knows what was waiting for him in the dead of night.

"Miss Sinclair is aware of our nightly excursions," Mr. Danbury said. "So far, that is the extent of her knowledge. I'll need you to stay with her tonight. I need to be certain she is safe."

Anna had the sudden urge to protest, an urge to ride out with him and confront whatever evil lurked in the darkness.

Tristan shook his head. "But I don't understand. She won't come to any harm in the monastery."

"I can't explain it all now," he said, no doubt referring to what she had told him about Victor.

There was a sudden flurry behind her: shouting and jeering. She clutched her chest fearing the man in question had risen from an earthy grave to seek his revenge. Anna breathed a sigh as a group of dancers pushed past them, waving their handkerchiefs and jingling their bells.

"Perhaps we should all head home," Mr. Danbury suggested, his tone revealing a hint of apprehension.

Tristan nodded. "There's nothing of any interest here. Lenard has spent the afternoon serving ale. With so many people coming into the village, it's hard to pick out strangers from abroad."

Strangers from abroad!

Anna's heart lurched, and she grabbed Mr. Danbury's arm as her frantic gaze met his. "I knew it. You really do think Victor's accomplice has come looking for me. You think he's here. Watching. Waiting. That's who you're searching for at night."

Mr. Danbury leant forward until his soft breath breezed across her cheek. "When I go out each night, I am not looking for Victor's accomplice," he whispered against her ear. "I am looking for criminals. I'm looking for smugglers."

CHAPTER 7

"Smugglers?" Miss Sinclair gasped as Marcus took her by the arm and escorted her towards the stables. It was not wise to discuss their assignment anywhere other than in the privacy of the chapter house. "You mean there really is no one lurking outside the monastery ready to exact their revenge for Victor's death?"

"Not that I'm aware of," Marcus replied. "And I scour the area nightly searching for anything suspicious."

"Forgive me for sounding obtuse," Tristan said, striding along with them. "But who in blazes is Victor? And I thought you said it was better for Anna if she knew nothing of our assignment."

He had said that.

But the look of fear in her eyes when she thought Victor's man had come looking for her, stabbed at his heart. It also occurred to him that wallowing in blissful ignorance was far more dangerous and posed a greater risk to her safety.

"If Lenard knows we suspect he's involved in nefarious activities, he may use any means necessary to guarantee our silence," Marcus countered. Indeed, some men would think nothing of taking another's life to save their own scrawny neck. "It is safer for Miss Sinclair if she knows who to trust should such an occasion arise."

Miss Sinclair gave a weary sigh. "Heavens, Lord Danesfield believes he has sent me to a place of sanctuary." She glanced over her shoulder before whispering, "I assume he knows nothing of your plan to spy on smugglers?"

"No," Marcus replied. "Had Dane known, I'm sure he would have thought twice about sending you here. But we'll discuss it further when we return to the monastery."

The groom met them upon their approach and led them to their horses. Tristan stepped forward to assist Miss Sinclair into the saddle, and she gave him one of her sweet smiles, one she rarely expressed in Marcus' company.

Marcus watched every movement, searching for the subtle touch that conveyed Tristan's innermost feelings. Had his friend's heart finally healed after five torturous years? Did it swell with affection for another—for Anna Sinclair—for the woman who caused Marcus' heart to beat a little faster, too?

"Are you comfortable?" Tristan asked, gazing up into her dazzling blue eyes.

"I am now. Thank you for your assistance, Mr. Wells."

She gave another one of her precious smiles, and Marcus groaned inwardly.

Feeling something he could only define as irritation, Marcus edged his horse forward. "I'll meet you back at the monastery." He dug his heels in, didn't bother to wait for a reply and cantered away without a nod or a word.

It was rude of him.

He should have waited.

But damn it all, he didn't like the sense of vulnerability he felt in her presence.

Tristan would watch over their guest. He would keep Miss Sinclair company with his witty quips, pristine clothes and fine noble features. Marcus had more important things to attend to. He needed to alert Coombes as soon as the smugglers prepared to set sail. Either the revenue ship would capture them off the coast and seize the contraband or his man from the Custom House would be ready as soon as they landed on English soil.

Upon his return to the monastery, Marcus stabled his horse and marched towards the chapter house. When the time was right, Lenard's men would move quickly. Marcus needed to be ready, and so he sat behind his desk with the intention of writing a letter to Coombes.

As he scrawled his missive, his attention was drawn to the eerie silence pervading the room. Ironically, he found it far too distracting.

He glanced at the clock on the mantel. Tristan and Miss Sinclair should have been back by now. Perhaps they had decided to stop and admire the scenery or wander down to the coastline to paddle their toes in the ice-cold water. He imagined her screaming and laughing as the waves chased her heels. Resentment roused its ugly head again, goading his mind to conjure a whole host of illicit images.

Jumping out of the chair as though the thing had caught fire, he brushed his hand through his hair.

Bloody hell.

He would punch Dane firmly in his gut when he saw him next. Never in his life had he experienced such inner turmoil.

Part of him wanted to put the delectable Miss Sinclair on the next ship back to England. Part of him wanted to cover her sweet body with his and forget the rest of the world existed.

Striding from the chapter house and through the garth, he made his way out of the door on the west side and scoured the lush green landscape.

Damn it. He would have to go back and search for them. By God, if he found them happily at their leisure he would unleash the Devil's wrath on the pair of them.

Pacing back and forth for a few minutes, he decided to walk as far as the gate. When he reached the gate, he decided to walk for another five minutes. That's all the time he would give them.

As he strode along the dusty road, mumbling and cursing at his own stupidity, he spotted their horses. Breaking into a jog, he raced down to the grassy verge to find Miss Sinclair sitting on the ground, leaning back against a tree. With her face white and ashen he knew something was wrong.

"What the hell happened?" He struggled to hide the panic in his voice.

"I … I came off my horse," Miss Sinclair said, wincing as she tried to move her leg.

Guilt stabbed a sharp spear into his chest.

"We were trying to keep pace with you," Tristan said, his tone revealing his reproof.

Marcus knelt down beside her, torn between wanting to pat her legs and being too damn scared to touch her. "Is anything broken?"

"No." She shook her head. "I'm just a little bruised. It's my fault. I haven't ridden in years and should not have pushed myself so hard."

Marcus sighed. It was his fault for listening to the jealous jibes of his inner voice. "I should have waited. I'm sorry."

Even Tristan's eyes widened at the sound of his apology. And by God, his friend would take great pleasure in teasing him for it later.

"Can you stand?" Marcus asked, showing genuine concern.

"I don't know." She shuffled forward a touch. "Could you lend me your arm for a moment?"

"Of course. Tristan, take Miss Sinclair's other arm." When his friend made no reply, Marcus glanced back over his shoulder to find Tristan examining her saddle. "Tristan!"

"Sorry, what did you want me to do?"

"Can you take one arm and I'll take the other? We'll support her weight until we know for certain nothing is broken."

Tristan nodded and came to stand at Miss Sinclair's right side. With them both kneeling beside her, she draped her arms around their shoulders as Marcus slid his other arm around her waist.

"On the count of three?" Tristan suggested.

Marcus nodded, and they lifted her up to her feet.

"It's my right leg," she said, hopping as she attempted to place her foot flat on the ground. "I'm certain it's not broken. It just feels a little tender that's all. See, I can hobble on it."

"Still, it's best not to take any chances." Marcus jerked his head towards the horses. "Tristan, if you lead the horses back, I'll carry Miss Sinclair."

"Carry me?" she gasped. "No, no, it won't be necessary. I can manage."

Marcus did not give her another chance to argue. As Tristan stepped away, he hauled Miss Sinclair up into his arms despite her squeal of protest, taking care not to hold her right leg as he did so.

As soon as he'd done it, he knew it was a mistake. Left with no choice but to wrap her arms around his neck, she pressed her supple body into his, and it took a tremendous amount of effort not to groan. Tristan seemed oblivious to his predicament as he took the reins and led the way back.

"You should put me down," she said, her face so close to his that he could feel her breath breeze over him. "I'm too heavy to carry all the way back to the monastery."

"Nonsense." His masculine pride refused to accept her reasoning. "I've carried a man twice your weight two miles or more through terrain far more unstable than this."

Perhaps fearing she might fall from his grasp, she tightened her grip around his neck. "Am I hurting you?"

"No." He was too busy worrying about the burning heat

racing through his body; he was too busy imagining a scene where he carried her up to his bed. "But you don't have to hold me so tight. I'm not going to drop you."

When they came upon the old rusty gate, he breathed a sigh.

As soon as they'd crossed the bridge, Tristan stopped. "I'll take the horses round. But when you've got a moment, can I speak to you in the stables?"

"I'll help Miss Sinclair to her room and then I'll be right down."

Tristan's brusque tone disturbed him. Perhaps his friend intended to berate him for leaving them behind. Perhaps he wanted to confess to there being more to his relationship with Anna Sinclair than simply friends.

"You don't need to carry me upstairs," Miss Sinclair said as they stopped at the bottom step. "I need to use my leg else it will only pain me all the more."

The woman's words were logical, and besides, carrying her to her chamber filled his head with thoughts of seduction.

"I'll put you down. Keep one arm around me for support until you feel ready to stand on your own."

She nodded, wincing as she anticipated the movement causing some pain.

"It's not as bad as I thought," she said, placing her foot on the floor, "although I'll probably have an ugly purple bruise on my thigh."

Marcus closed his eyes briefly and inhaled. Why did she have to mention her thigh? An image of him examining the bruise while her lithe leg hung over his bare shoulder, burst into his mind.

"How … how did you come to fall?" He coughed to clear his throat as his voice sounded strained.

"I don't know. We were riding rather fast." She managed to climb the next step with a little more ease. "And then I just slipped from the saddle."

By the time they reached the top, she could walk without support. He opened the door to her chamber and stepped back to allow her to enter. "When Selene returns, I'll get her to make a poultice to help reduce any bruising. Do you need any help getting into bed?"

"No." As she shook her head, her blue eyes flashed with a mild look of panic. "And thank you for your help. I think I'll walk around the room for a while to ease the stiffness."

Marcus would need to walk five miles or more to reduce the stiffness in a certain part of his anatomy. He inclined his head. "If you need anything, I shall be downstairs."

She smiled, and his heart lurched. "Thank you, Mr. Danbury."

Tristan was waiting for him in the stable, sitting on a wooden crate and staring at the floor. He looked up and jumped to his feet as Marcus entered.

"Look, I know what you're going to say," Marcus began, "and you're right. I should not have ridden off like that. I should have done the gentlemanly thing and waited."

Tristan snorted. "Since when have you been known to do the gentlemanly thing?" He strode over to Miss Sinclair's horse and ran his hand down over the girth strap. "But here, you need to see this."

Marcus walked over to examine the tack. Where the strap ran under the barrel of the horse's chest, the leather had split. The two pieces were only held together by the line of stitching on the outer edge. "It looks as though it's been cut through with a knife or a similarly sharp object."

"That is my theory," Tristan replied. "But why not cut through the whole strap?"

Marcus put his hands on the saddle and tested the manoeuvrability. "Because we would have noticed the strap hanging loose. This way the saddle is stable enough to sit on but unstable when riding at speed."

Tristan shook his head. "It still makes no sense. Do you think the culprit knew it was Anna's horse? And if so, what reason would he have for hoping she would fall?"

Marcus drew his hand down his face, massaged his jaw with his thumb and forefinger. "It has to be connected to Lenard. Someone must have overheard our conversation. Perhaps the groom led them to our horses. I'm certain the purpose of the act was merely to frighten us."

"I find it hard to believe Lenard knows of our involvement. Or that he even had time to tamper with the strap." Tristan paused for a moment. "What of this Victor fellow? I assume he's the reason Dane sent Anna here."

"Victor is dead." Marcus refused to reveal he had met his demise by Miss Sinclair's hand. "And I do not believe his accomplice, if such a man exists, is searching for Miss Sinclair."

Tristan shrugged. "So what do you propose we do now?"

"We will tell Miss Sinclair what we suspect and continue with our assignment."

"Tell her? Surely she will only worry."

"She is stronger than you think." Marcus suspected her life with Victor had been far from pleasant. Miss Sinclair was one of the world's survivors. "We will tell her the truth. Dane would not have sent her to us if she was not to be trusted."

Tristan nodded. "I would trust you with my life, Marcus. And I shall trust your decision in this."

Marcus grabbed his friend's shoulder: a masculine gesture of affection. "Miss Sinclair has been sent to us for a reason." Yes, to torture him with her luscious body and kind overtures. To force him to lie awake in bed each night with a throbbing cock and a guilty conscience. "Perhaps she could work with us. After all, she has some skill when it comes to distracting the hearts and minds of men."

Of that he was certain.

CHAPTER 8

Despite pleading with Mr. Danbury to allow Tristan to accompany him on his nightly reconnaissance, he had insisted on going out alone.

The hollow feeling in Anna's chest, which she attributed to fear, did not subside. After all, someone had deliberately cut through the strap on her saddle. Someone lurked out there in the shadows ready to wreak mischief or exact their revenge. Anna had heard tales of smugglers dragging loose-tongued witnesses from their beds and stringing them up from the highest bough. Whether the mysterious culprit was guilty of smuggling casks of brandy or innocent women from the streets of London remained to be seen.

For once, Tristan's jolly countenance did not alleviate her melancholic mood. Feigning a throbbing ache in her thigh, the bruise being less painful than she had anticipated, Anna went up to her bedchamber to watch from the window until Mr. Danbury returned. If he insisted on going out again tomorrow night, she would demand Tristan went, too.

Minutes stretched into hours.

What on earth was he doing out in the darkness?

With her head resting on her arm, she heard the sound of horse's hooves clipping over the bridge before she saw him approach. Whistling a tune as he rode past her window, she scanned his muscular form. He sat straight, not hunched forward or clutching his side. And so, convinced he had not come to any harm, she breathed a sigh and settled into bed.

When she eventually fell asleep, her dreams were plagued by terrifying visions of a brutal sea battle. She fled to the upper deck just as heavy cannon fire hit the wooden boards, splintering them easily upon impact. The floor beneath her tipped, tilting to the right, so she was forced to hold her arms out to steady her balance.

Victor's hideous form appeared through the billowing smoke. The smell of charred wood reminded her of the cheroots he puffed on daily. He strode over to her in his usual pompous way, grasped her chin with his bony fingers and pushed her backwards. She tumbled into the sea, sinking into the icy depths, her long hair fanning out in the water like a peacock's tail feathers, her wide eyes sad and soulless as she clutched at nothing.

Anna woke with a start.

The morning sun streamed in through her window, heralding the start of a new day and an end to the torturous nightmares. Thank goodness she had no mirror in her room as her lids were surely puffy and swollen from lack of sleep.

Throwing on her clothes and washing in the cold water left in the bowl, she made her way downstairs. With the refectory deserted, Anna knew Selene would not be far away.

"Good morning, Selene," Anna said, finding the woman making bread in the kitchen. "Did you enjoy the fair?"

Selene's curious gaze drifted over her. "*Oui*, *madame*. How is your leg? Did the poultice help?"

"It did," Anna nodded. "Although the smell was rather

unpleasant, something akin to rotting leaves and wet grass. But it took the swelling down and now I hardly know the bruise is there."

Selene raised her chin in acknowledgement. "Did you come to eat?" she said, turning back to knead the dough.

"Yes. But don't worry. I'll help myself to bread and some of your strawberry preserve."

"No," Selene cried, meeting Anna's gaze. "Mr. Danbury will think I am lazy. He will not like guests serving themselves."

"I am hardly a guest." Anna chuckled. "Mr. Danbury has me digging the flower beds until my hands are blistered and sore. I'm sure he won't mind me cutting a slice of bread."

Selene tutted, sighed and turned back to her dough. "Very well. But you must be quick."

Feeling as though she was intruding, Anna hurried about cutting the bread, eager to leave the kitchen. She wondered if Selene knew of her life back in London. Perhaps the woman disapproved of how she'd made her living and used her inexperience with the language to hide her disdain.

If Anna continued to feel uncomfortable in her presence, she would broach the subject.

After eating her breakfast and finishing her chores, she washed her hands and headed out into the garth. She longed to sit and feel the warm rays of the sun touch her cheeks and treasured the hour she spent there every day.

Anna's cheerful smile faded when she spotted Tristan slumped forward on her favourite bench, his head buried in his hands.

"Tristan." She approached with hesitant feet. "Are you well?"

He glanced up, a mop of golden hair hindering his vision. "No, Anna, I am not well at all," he said in a tone as solemn as his countenance.

"Can I get you anything? A tonic, or something cold to drink?"

"There is no cure for what ails me," he replied cryptically.

Anna had never seen him look so distraught. "May I sit or would you prefer I left you alone?"

Tristan straightened, brushed his hair from his brow and shuffled further along the bench. "Please sit. Perhaps you will be able to offer words of encouragement, know of a way to soothe my wounds."

"I do not wish to pry." She sat at his side. "But you know you may speak freely to me. You know I would never break a confidence."

"You have been a good friend to me these last weeks, and I am grateful for it. Marcus will need a friend, too. Promise me you will take supper with him, that you'll keep him company."

Anna snorted. "You make it sound as though you're leaving."

The drawn-out silence gave weight to her flippant comment.

Tristan swallowed visibly. "I must return to London as a matter of urgency." In a sudden outburst, he jumped up from the bench and swiped the air with his clenched fist. "Damn it all. I vowed never to return. It's all a bloody mess." He glanced at her with sad eyes. "Forgive my rants and curses. But you don't know what this means."

Struggling to follow his train of thought, Anna reached up and grasped his elbow. "Sit down, Tristan." She spoke softly. "Sit down and tell me what troubles you. Tell me what's so awful about going home."

With a heavy sigh, he dropped back into the wooden seat. "It's Isabella," he said, shaking his head, his eyes wide in disbelief.

Anna threaded her arm through his and hugged it. "Is she your sister, a friend or something more?"

"Some would say she is all of those things." He gazed up at the cloudless sky and sighed wearily. "As far as my father was concerned, she was a sister. But I have never seen her as such. She became his ward after losing her parents. And I have loved her for as long as I can remember."

Love existed in varying degrees and depths.

"When you say love, do you mean you love her as a man would a woman?" Anna clarified.

Tristan nodded. "She has claimed my heart and soul. She should have been my wife, but my father forbade it. Now, she is married to another, and I swore I would rather die than bear witness to her betrayal."

Anna's heart went out to him. She would rather live in ignorance than be denied true love. What could be life's greatest gift could also be a tragic burden.

Tristan turned to face her. "Have you ever been in love?"

The question shocked her. For some bizarre reason, an image of Mr. Danbury flashed into her mind, and she quickly dismissed it.

"Good heavens, no. No, I have never been in love," she said. "I am far too cynical and have witnessed the true depth of a lover's betrayal." Most of the gentlemen who frequented Labelles were married. Indeed, she recalled one particular patron who entertained two of her girls on the night of his wedding.

"Then you are much wiser than I."

Anna doubted that. She had not been wise enough to avoid Victor's cunning trap.

"How long has it been since you last spoke to her?"

Tristan exhaled. "Five years. We were eloping when my father caught up with us on the road north. He dragged us both home, despite our protests. When I woke the next morning, he had taken Isabella away with him. Sometime later, she wrote to me and told me she had married Lord Fernall."

"I'm so sorry, Tristan." Anna had heard many tales of ladies tricked into marriage; perhaps Isabella had suffered a similar fate. "I don't mean to be insensitive, but have you never found love with another?"

"No. Although my mind and body function in the present, it is as though my heart and soul are stuck in the past."

Anna smiled to hide the sudden wave of sadness his words roused. "I do know how it feels to be detached from reality." When Victor had forced her to work at Labelles, she'd left her heart and soul safely back at her home in the country. "But you have not said why you must return."

Tristan exhaled deeply once more and closed his eyes briefly. "My brother …" He paused and shook his head. "My brother has died without issue. You are looking at the new Viscount Morford. My mother insists I am to return home to take my rightful place as head of the family."

Anna was left utterly speechless. The poor man looked so lost and forlorn. "I am truly sorry to hear of your brother's death. But your mother is right. The *ton* needs strong, selfless gentlemen to take the lead. You are a good and loyal person, Tristan, and will serve your family well."

"It is not the life I wanted or envisaged for myself. And I cannot bear the thought of leaving Marcus here alone. I do not wish to speak ill, but he is more of a brother to me than Andrew ever was."

Anna's heart lurched as she imagined Mr. Danbury stomping along the cloisters with no one to talk to, no one to help him on his nightly crusades.

"What did Mr. Danbury say when you told him?"

"That's part of the problem," Tristan said. "I haven't told him. The letter arrived yesterday, but I recognised the seal and only opened it this morning."

Mr. Danbury would console him, ease his conscience and convey nothing of the inner turmoil hidden inside.

"Come." Anna stood and pulled him to his feet. "Let me

wish you well. Then we will go together and break the news to Mr. Danbury."

"I cannot ask you to do that."

"You didn't ask. I offered." She held out her arms, and they hugged—as friends, as though they were kin. "I will stay at the monastery as long as Mr. Danbury needs me or wants me here, although that may only amount to one more day."

Tristan smiled. "He does like you, you know. For the last few years, I've been suggesting he goes down to the fair, yet he's not come within a mile of the place."

"Selene did seem rather shocked he'd agreed to go. I would go as far as to say the woman is terrified of him."

"As I told you when you arrived, his growl is worse than his bite. But wait until he discovers I'm a peer. You'll want to put your fingers in your ears for that."

Marcus hovered at the door of the chapter house and watched them embrace. Tristan and Miss Sinclair cared for one another. That much was obvious. He could see a glimmer of tenderness in his friend's eyes when he spoke to her. During their brief conversation, she had touched his arm numerous times.

Bloody hell.

The whole thing was driving him insane. Part of him would be glad when Miss Sinclair left. Then they could return to how things used to be. To a time when he didn't feel jealousy slithering through him leaving a poisonous trail in its wake.

As they stepped apart, Marcus closed the door gently with both hands and marched round to his desk. Last night, he had followed two men from Lenard's inn to an abandoned cottage set back in a copse just a ten-minute walk from the cliff edge. He'd followed the cliff as it sloped down before breaking to reveal the wide walkway leading to the shore.

His orders were specific. Alert Coombes at the first sign of Lenard's men loading their contraband into the boat. Now he knew where they kept their booty it was only a matter of time before they set sail.

The rapping on the door stole his attention. When Tristan entered, accompanied by Miss Sinclair, Marcus' chest grew tight. They had come together to tell him something important. A quick glance at their sorrowful expressions sent his thoughts into disarray.

"Tristan. Miss Sinclair." He gave a curt nod, kept his tone even and focused on keeping his composure.

"Shouldn't you bow to a lord when he enters the room?" Tristan said with a chuckle. He glanced at Miss Sinclair, who hovered at his shoulder. "Get ready to put your fingers in your ears."

Marcus sneered. "You know I wouldn't even spit on a lord let alone bow to one."

"What did I tell you? He despises peers."

"I am certain his feelings will change," Miss Sinclair nodded.

"I am still here. And no, my feelings on the matter will never change."

"But you're friends with Lord Danesfield?" she replied with a shrug.

"Dane is the exception to the rule."

Miss Sinclair smiled. "Well, then you may add one more exception to your list. Tristan has just discovered he is the new Viscount Morford."

Marcus shot out of the chair so fast the room spun, and he struggled to focus. He could feel the blood drain from his face, pooling thick and heavy in his throat. "Good God. Andrew is … he is dead?"

Tristan nodded. "I know nothing more than that."

Marcus came around the desk and put his hands on Tristan's

shoulders. “I am truly sorry, Tristan. Is there anything I can do? I assume your mother and sister wish you to return home for a time?”

Tristan shook his head. “Marcus, they want me to return home indefinitely.”

Marcus’ hands slipped from Tristan’s shoulders. It felt like a huge hollow cavern had opened up in his chest. They had been as close as brothers these last five years. Despite letting jealousy take root over Tristan’s friendship with Miss Sinclair, he loved him—would die to save him.

“I see.” They were the only words Marcus could form. A world filled with nothing but loneliness and solitude opened up before him.

“I don’t know what to do.” Tristan shrugged and glanced at Miss Sinclair. “I can’t leave you to deal with Lenard on your own. And who will watch over Anna while you’re out at night?”

Marcus pushed aside all his selfish thoughts. “Your family must come before either of us or the assignment.”

Tristan knew him well enough to know that nothing would get in the way of their assignment. Marcus would find a way to get the job done.

“What if I go home for a few days or so? I could be back here in a week. Then I’ll stay until we’ve dealt with Lenard.”

“Lenard could make his move tonight.” Marcus understood his friend’s desire to ease his conscience, but he suspected he would complete their assignment before Tristan returned. “I doubt he’ll wait more than a few days before heading out. No. Forget about Lenard. You have enough to concern yourself with. Miss Sinclair and I will find a way to manage.”

“I agree,” Miss Sinclair said, stepping forward to stand at his shoulder. Under such grim circumstances, he found the gesture oddly reassuring. “It will fall to us to deal with things in your absence, Tristan. I’m certain we will manage perfectly well.”

He wondered if she truly believed that or if the words were said purely to placate Tristan. She spoke with the confidence of a duchess, and it occurred to him she knew how to take control of difficult situations. The leery lords of London were not easy men to deal with, particularly when randy and in their cups.

"I will be Mr. Danbury's partner," she continued boldly. "I will help him in any way I can."

Marcus cleared his throat and stepped back to face her. "Excuse me?"

She smiled. "I'll partner you this evening."

The words roused visions of her partnering him in a much more amorous activity, a wild and erotic coupling that satisfied the lust clawing at his needy body.

"Good Lord," Tristan blurted, his wide eyes revealing more than shock. "You cannot be serious. Do you know what Lenard's men will do to you if they discover you're an informer?"

Miss Sinclair lifted her chin and gave a look defiant enough to bring any nobleman to his knees. It confirmed Marcus' suspicion that she had rallied her alter ego, Madame Labelle, to do her bidding.

"Suffice to say, I will not go into the tiresome details of past encounters," she said with an air of superiority. "I may not be skilled in the use of a sword or pistol. But I am resourceful, sharp-witted and loyal to a fault when I believe in the cause."

Marcus resisted the urge to clap. He admired her gumption, knew she would not falter when it mattered. She had neglected to inform Tristan of her experience with a blade. Indeed, he felt privileged to be the one she'd confided in. She had killed a man out of necessity and in that respect would be a useful ally.

"So," Marcus began. He gave an exaggerated wave to feign a degree of disapproval, yet he was confident he could manage the minx and keep her safe. "Let me understand you. What you propose is an alliance, a merging of efforts."

"Precisely," she nodded.

Tristan glared at Marcus. "You're not considering it?"

Marcus ignored him. Hot blood pumped through his veins at the thought of spending the lonely nights in her company. "If you intend to fill Tristan's boots in his absence, it will mean taking commands from me."

She would know exactly who was in charge here. In order to protect her, he had to trust in her ability to follow orders.

She arched a mocking brow. "You are to command me in the field, Mr. Danbury, nothing more."

"Agreed," he snapped in his eagerness to seal their deal.

"What?" Tristan grabbed Marcus' arm in a bid to get his full attention. "Have you lost your mind?"

For the first time since her arrival, she presented Tristan with a scowl. "I am more than capable, my lord."

Marcus felt the sting in her recognition of Tristan's new title.

"Anna, please," Tristan said in a softer tone. "You're making it awfully hard for me to leave knowing you'll be out there, dicing with danger."

She straightened as her expression darkened. "Dicing with danger? I have diced with the Devil, and I am the one still standing."

Excitement bubbled away in Marcus' chest. He put his hand on Tristan's shoulder. "I have not lost a man yet, and I do not propose to do so now. Have faith in my ability to get the job done."

Tristan sighed and drew his palm down his face. "Do you still have a flask of brandy in your desk?"

Marcus smirked. "You look as though you need a bottle. Help yourself to it while I discuss the particulars with Miss Sinclair."

"The particulars?" She stepped closer, the sweet scent of almonds drifting over him.

"To begin with, we shall dispense with all formality. You will call me Marcus."

"Then you must call me Anna."

Marcus put his hand to his chin in thoughtful contemplation as his gaze scanned her dull dress. "Agreed. I will call you Anna in private, but something more masculine when you don breeches to ride out with me at night." When her eyes grew as wide as trenchers, he added, "We do not want the smugglers to know you're a woman."

Tristan mumbled something as he sat in the chair behind them.

Miss Sinclair put her hands on her hips and huffed. "What did you have in mind?"

"Something that's easy to remember. Something short, something fitting." He knew just the thing. "I have it. I shall call you Ned during our assignment."

"Ned? Ned! Is that the best you can do?"

Marcus pursed his lips. Despite feeling a deep sadness over Tristan's impending departure, Miss Sinclair would help to ease the burden. "It reminds me of a horse I once had, so I'm unlikely to forget it."

When a smirk touched the corners of her lips, he should have known her sharp wits were about to come into play.

"You believe it is wise to disguise one's identity when informing on criminal activity?"

He gave a firm nod. "I do."

"Then I shall also refer to you by another name during our assignment. It would not be wise for me to call out your name in the darkness. One never knows who is lurking in the shrubbery, listening to our conversation."

"She's right," Tristan remarked. "You can't argue with her logic."

Marcus sat on the edge of his desk and folded his arms

across his chest. “Let me guess. You’ve decided you’ll call me Milo, after a mangy dog.”

“Oh, no.” She shook her head. “I would never demean you in such a way. I think I will call you Rupert.”

“Rupert?” Heavens, the name gave him chills, but he hid it well. “After a beloved family member I presume.”

“No.” She chuckled. “After a pompous lord filled with his own self-importance.”

CHAPTER 9

Having shared an early supper with Tristan, the event more subdued than previous meals enjoyed at the long crude table, Anna decided to accompany Mr. Danbury as he walked his friend to the gate.

They stopped a few feet from the entrance.

"You will write and let us know how you fare?" Anna rubbed Tristan's arm affectionately, fearing an embrace would result in her shedding tears.

"You know I will,"

Mr. Danbury pulled Tristan to his chest and patted him on the back. "It's not going to be the same around here without your jolly antics. I fear I shall be more solemn than ever."

"I doubt that's even possible." Tristan laughed, but it failed to reach his eyes, and she knew he found it hard to say goodbye. "Try to be a little more hospitable in my absence. Conversation can be quite stimulating you know."

"Miss Sinclair and I are going down to the village inn this evening," Mr. Danbury said with a smirk. "We can converse over a mug of ale. I can't be any more hospitable than that."

Anna turned to him and narrowed her gaze. "When you

mentioned we would be going out this evening, I didn't think we'd be going to the inn."

Mr. Danbury shrugged. "I thought we'd discuss it later. As I recall, you did agree to follow my command."

"Then I assume we'll be working." Anna could feel a nervous energy bouncing back and forth between them.

"Would you follow my command if I said no? Would you come with me if I said our visit had nothing to do with the assignment?"

"I think you know the answer, Mr. Danbury."

"Marcus. You agreed to call me Marcus."

Anna exhaled deeply.

The next few days would be interesting. Working with Mr. Danbury would result in one of two things. Either they would become firm friends, trust one another implicitly, share their deepest, darkest secrets. Or, they would grow to despise one another until it became impossible to be in the same room without revealing their contempt.

Tristan smiled. "Part of me wishes I was staying just to witness the outcome of this war of wills."

"I feel it may be a long drawn out battle," Marcus said with a chuckle. Anna was about to protest, when he added, "One where brute strength may be overthrown by a woman's intelligence and cunning wiles."

She felt her cheeks flame at his obvious compliment. Good heavens, she had seen wrinkly old lords spread naked on a bed. She had seen grown men dressed as young girls, heard the growl of a man's pleasure accompanied by the loud crack of a whip. Why one silly remark should make her feel light-headed and giddy was beyond her.

Tristan shook Marcus' hand. "Well, I wish you luck with Lenard. Don't do anything foolish. Observe their movements and report it. Nothing more."

"You know me. I always seem to be in the wrong place at the wrong time."

Anna watched the exchange with keen interest. She imagined Mr. Danbury was a law unto himself; there were no restrictions or boundaries when it came to doing what he felt was right. Not many men possessed such a quality. Some would frown on his unconventional approach to things. Surprisingly, Anna found she admired him all the more for it.

Tristan stepped in front of her and brought her hand to his lips. "Remember what I said when you arrived, about the lion's lair."

Anna smiled. "It is as I suspected. It is the lair of a fluffy kitten in the guise of a ferocious beast."

Tristan nodded. "Always keep that in mind and you will do well here."

"If you happen to see Lord Danesfield on your return, will you ask how long I'm to stay?" It could well be that she developed an aversion to kittens and it would be helpful to know she could escape back to London if necessary.

"Of course," Tristan nodded. He stepped closer and embraced her purely to whisper, "Take care of him. He's not as strong as he looks."

The words made her heart flutter. She couldn't help but glance at Mr. Danbury's muscled shoulders filling his shirt. Strong did not go nearly far enough to convey the power emanating from such a robust physique. Anna imagined many women had run their hands over the chiselled contours, felt the warmth radiate from his bare skin. It shouldn't matter to her, but oddly it did.

"Enough of this soppy sentiment," Mr. Danbury chided, and he held the reins on Tristan's horse while he mounted. "Send my regards to your mother and sister."

Tristan shuffled in his saddle then gave a firm nod. "Wish me luck. I'm going to need it. I think I'd rather walk into Lenard's inn shouting ‘where are the smugglers?’ than step into a crowded ballroom after all these years.”

“I’d rather tie an anchor to my ankle and throw myself overboard.” Marcus laughed, the deep creases around his eyes making him appear carefree, more appealing.

“You’re supposed to make me feel better.” Tristan tipped his hat. “I’ll see you both soon and stay out of trouble.”

They stood side-by-side at the gate and watched the dust settle as Tristan rode far from view. Anna felt a deep ache in her chest. Surprisingly, it had nothing to do with her own feelings regarding Tristan’s departure. From the sound of Mr. Danbury’s strained breathing, she knew he would miss his friend terribly, and it roused a need to offer comfort.

“Come.” She touched his sleeve lightly. “I will pour you a drink while you tell me why we’re going to the inn tonight.”

In her experience, distracting the mind was the best way to cope with feelings of dejection.

He glanced down at her fingers. She had forgotten how unsightly they were and so hid them behind the folds of her skirt.

“If you’re to assist me with the assignment, you won’t have time to do chores.” He struggled to make eye contact, his gaze drifting past her shoulder. “I’ll tell Andre you’ll be taking over Tristan’s administration duties in his absence.”

“Is it my hands?” she asked, sensing guilt played a part in his decision.

“They need time to heal.” When he looked at her, his warm brown eyes did reveal a trace of guilt. “Have you been applying the balm?”

She shrugged. “When I remember.”

The corners of his mouth twitched. “Only once then.”

“Yes, only once.”

He inhaled deeply, the air causing his chest and shoulders to expand before her eyes. “You can forget pouring me a drink.

Bring the balm to the chapter house and we'll deal with your hands while I tell you of our plans."

Anyone else might think he'd made a quick recovery following Tristan's departure, that his sullen mood had been feigned for his friend's benefit. Anna knew he relied on his domineering countenance to distract from dealing with difficult emotions.

"That sounds very much like a command, Mr. Danbury," she said in jest hoping to lighten his spirits.

"It is a request, Anna. An offer of help, a friendly gesture of assistance."

Her heart raced at the use of her given name. It sounded different falling from his lips as opposed to Tristan's.

"Then I accept your friendly gesture, Marcus."

She turned to walk back to the monastery, and he followed her lead. Deciding to offer a friendly gesture of her own, she threaded her arm through his. He did not protest, only stopping once to glance back over his shoulder.

When she returned to the chapter house with her pot of salve, she found Marcus lounging behind his desk. His hands were clasped behind his head as he stared at nothing.

As she entered the room, he straightened. "Did you bring the balm?"

Anna nodded, sat in the chair opposite and placed the pot on his desk. "Selene said I'm supposed to apply it before bed, but I don't suppose it matters."

A sinful smile touched his lips. "It would not do to fall into bed so early. Not unless one had things in mind other than sleep."

Perhaps he assumed the madam of a brothel enjoyed salacious banter as a dressmaker desired talking of ribbons and pins.

"Then you have discovered my naughty secret, Marcus." When his eyes widened, she added, "There is nothing I love more than climbing into bed in the afternoon to read a few pages of my favourite book."

His smile softened his features. "I have often thought I should read more."

"Then I suggest you start with something a little less complicated. Something that takes less effort and is guaranteed to please."

"Perhaps pleasure is more satisfying when it comes from something one believes is unattainable, far beyond the realms of one's capabilities."

Despite her initial frustration, she found their verbal sparring highly entertaining. "Is it not better to eat the apple from the lower bough than to risk falling empty-handed from the top?"

"They are words spoken by a woman who has never climbed a tree. Don't you know the apples at the top are far juicier? The sweet taste becomes ingrained in your memory, never to be forgotten."

A faint flicker of desire ignited. It was something she never expected to feel. How could she when all the men she'd ever met had been rotten scoundrels? Although since making their acquaintance, Lord Danesfield and Tristan had proved to be worthy gentlemen. And she couldn't forget Morgan. The man paid to do Victor's bidding had sacrificed his life to save her.

"You're right," she said, her morbid memories bringing an end to the entertainment. "I have never climbed a tree and, therefore, do not speak from experience."

He raised an enquiring brow but said nothing. Leaning forward, he took the pot and removed the lid before holding out his hand.

Anna stared at the rough skin where his fingers met his palm. She knew one thing: the man was not a hypocrite. "I think you could do with a pot of balm, too," she said, aware of the nervous edge to her tone.

"Give me your hand."

It sounded like a command, yet her heart fluttered softly in response.

A different sort of fear shrouded her, one vastly more dangerous, one threatening the protective shield she'd built around the tender organ. Her body reacted before her mind could decide what to do. Tentative fingers moved across the desk towards him. She tried to ignore the fire shooting through her veins as he wrapped his hand around hers.

He stared at her for a moment, his rich brown eyes penetrating her flimsy armour. "I'm told you rub it into the skin in circular motions."

Her pulse thumped hard at the base of her throat. "Yes. It helps to soak into the layers of the skin."

He put his fingers into the pot and scooped out a small amount of balm. "It may hurt a little," he said, dabbing some over her knuckles and a bit on each finger.

Anna winced as he began to rub in gentle, circular movements. A variety of smells permeated the air, and she focused on trying to identify them in a bid to ignore the sweet fire his touch roused.

"I can smell rosemary," she said, swallowing deeply.

He nodded and gave a low hum. "I can smell honey, too, and almonds. The combination is quite soothing to the mind."

Soothing?

Her mind darted about from one chaotic image to another. The sense of desperate longing escalated when he turned her hand over to massage her palm.

"You … you were going to tell me why we're visiting the inn tonight." There, a change of subject would soon dampen her ardour.

"Oh, yes. It occurred to me that your assistance might prove valuable." He did not look up at her until he had finished his ministrations and then he placed her hand gently on the desk. "If we're seen together regularly, it will not look so suspicious if someone should find us roaming the woods at night."

"But won't it look odd? I can't imagine there are many women willing to enter an inn full of drunken men." A strange foreboding settled over her. "Unless you want me to dress in breeches while you call me Ned."

He laughed. "Not tonight. Perhaps Ned can come visit tomorrow." He pointed at her arm. "Give me your other hand."

Incredulously, she obeyed, but her mind was too occupied to worry about his warm touch.

"We can sit outside the inn if you prefer. Go for a stroll in the vicinity. It will give me a chance to survey who enters the premises. No one will think to question the motives of a man entertaining his mistress."

"Mistress!" The heat smouldering inside her body rushed to her face, and she could feel her cheeks burn. "Do not think to presume—"

"I do not presume anything. I speak with the best interests of the assignment in mind. May I remind you, you were the one offering yourself up as the sacrificial lamb."

She snatched her hand away. "Yes. But Tristan looked so worried, so racked with guilt, I thought it the only option."

He sat back in the chair, folded his arms across his chest and gave a smug grin. "That's not entirely true now is it? You're used to taking control and, if I'm not mistaken, you're suffering from boredom. You wanted something to occupy your time other than digging up soil and picking herbs."

Anna couldn't argue with him. She had been desperate to find something useful to do. Something where she might prove her worth, the self-sacrifice a way of absolving the sins of the past.

"Can't you just say I'm your sister, come for a visit?"

He rubbed his chin, offered a look of thoughtful contemplation. "I suppose I could, but would the bastard son of an earl and his kitchen maid have kin? Of course, then it would look rather strange if I'm caught kissing you?"

Once again, Anna's thoughts were sent scattering like crisp leaves in the wind. She didn't know which revelation to address first. Marcus Danbury was the son of an earl and a kitchen maid? It explained everything. She sensed his contempt ran deeper than the social scars he'd been burdened with. The need to discover all of his darkest secrets burst forth. She wanted to understand him, delve deeper beneath his arrogant facade.

"Why on earth would you think we'd be caught kissing?" she said, deciding to deal with the other shocking revelation.

He moistened his lips. "Because I think we both know it is inevitable."

Anger flared. "Why, you conceited oaf. I should have guessed."

"Guessed what?"

"That the village simpleton would seek sanctuary in a monastery."

He sniggered. "Give me your hand and let me finish applying the balm." He reached across the desk and when she failed to abide by his request, he added, "Look, forget what I said. I spoke out of turn. It was foolish of me."

Anna raised her chin. "You didn't mean it then?"

His heated gaze lingered on her lips and the corner of his mouth twitched in amusement. "Just give me your hand and let me help you. I can't possibly entertain a mistress with the hands of a scullery maid."

CHAPTER 10

"We're only taking one horse?" Anna frowned as she pulled her cape tightly around her. "Where's the logic in that?"

The creature snorted wildly, mimicking her disgruntled tone and Marcus gave him a firm pat of reassurance.

"That's where you're wrong." He expected her to question his decision. In fact, he'd been looking forward to the opportunity of sparring words with her. "It is entirely logical. Firstly, with the intimacy of the act, people will assume there is an attachment between us." He couldn't resist the urge to tease her. "It will save me the trouble of kissing you."

"And save me the trouble of slapping you again." She huffed as she stuck her nose in the air. But his attention was captured by the way her turquoise-blue eyes twinkled in the darkness.

"Don't underestimate the power anger plays in the igniting of one's desire." He suppressed a snigger. "I've known many amorous interludes begin with heated words or a sharp slap."

"Well, you'll find nothing contradictory about me." She shook her head and sighed. "If I'm angry, you will know it. If passion burns in my chest, you can be certain it has nothing to do with your overbearing manner."

Marcus could spend every hour of the day bantering with her. She really was entertaining company, although she was wrong in her assessment. Everything about her posed an interesting contradiction. On one hand, she conveyed a strong, forthright approach. Yet there were many secrets buried beneath her open countenance. At times, she appeared as innocent as a girl making her debut. So much so, he found it hard to image her working in a house of ill repute.

One thing was certain. Marcus would enjoy unravelling the conflicting threads of her character.

He cleared his throat as he tried to maintain a serious tone. "I hate to mention it, but you did agree to follow my command. We are to be on a reconnaissance mission. As such, whatever we do tonight we do for king and country."

She gave a loud tut, a frustrated sound of surrender. Perhaps he would use the same line again as he wondered how far she would go in her duty to the Crown.

Anna folded her arms across her chest. "You implied there was another logical reason for riding out together? I assume it's a little more practical."

"Of course. If we need to escape quickly, for whatever reason, I cannot take the risk of you falling behind." He winced when he said it as her expression darkened. "This way we'll be together whatever happens."

"I don't know whether to be furious or flattered by your concern."

"Be flattered," he said nonchalantly. "Normally, I wouldn't give the matter much thought."

"That's a lie," she said, her face suddenly brightening as though she'd pricked him with the tip of her sabre because he'd been too slow to parry. "You told Tristan you've never lost a man."

Damn the woman.

He'd never admit it, but he feared she was too quick-witted for him.

Marcus ran his tongue over his bottom lip while he attempted to make a speedy recovery. "Judging by your curvaceous figure, I think it's fair to say you're no man."

She sighed again. "I'm not going to bother answering. At this rate, we will still be standing in the stable yard come morning. Perhaps we should be on our way."

"My thoughts exactly." Without another word he settled his hands on her narrow waist, ignoring her shriek as he hoisted her up onto the saddle. Climbing up behind her, he dug in his heels before she could protest further.

Now that he'd shuffled closer, and she'd been forced to snuggle into him to provide better stability whilst perched sideways on his saddle, he acknowledged that he hadn't been entirely honest with her.

There had been a third reason behind his decision to take only one horse.

It was a test—to see if his body could withstand the temptation of being pressed so closely against her. He had done it to see how she would react to his touch; whether he stood even the remotest chance of indulging his passion for her.

What was so damn frustrating was that she appeared impervious to the heat radiating from him, indifferent to the feel of his throbbing cock pressed against her hip. With her back rigid, her breathing calm and even, it made not a jot of difference to her steely composure.

His body, on the other hand, roared like a blasted inferno.

Sitting nestled between his thighs, she stared out at the passing countryside, which on a sunny day would not have been so surprising. Now the sun had set, the rolling fields and woodland looked like dull grey shadows beneath the inky sky. There was certainly nothing fascinating about the view. And with the chill in the air, he would have expected her to snuggle closer to his chest.

All was not lost, however.

After climbing down and tying the horse to the post in the village, Marcus offered his hand to her. She gave a curt nod: permission for him to touch her again and lower her to the ground. He did so slowly, letting her slide down the full length of his body, so close he could feel her sweet breath against his cheek.

Anna inhaled deeply, and he felt a shiver run through her.

It took a tremendous amount of effort not to jump up and punch the air. The fact she may desire him coupled with the illicit thoughts running through his head were almost his undoing.

Good God.

He was starting to think like a boy from the schoolroom. He sniggered at the thought. While his head might be lost in a hazy cloud of excitement and anticipation, when it came to their coupling, they would meet as skilled experts in the art of giving pleasure.

"We'll head straight to the inn, spend an hour or so there." When he took her hand and placed it in the crook of his arm, she made no protest. He cast a sidelong glance, noting the look of concentration dominating her countenance. "Remember, you are supposed to be my mistress. You should try to look as though you're enjoying the experience."

She turned to him. "What would you like me to do? Should I stroke your overinflated sense of importance? Drool at the sight of your muscular shoulders?"

Marcus smirked. She could stroke the only part of his anatomy he considered overinflated. "You think my shoulders are muscular. That's a start. Although I would rather you bite down on them while shuddering with the effects of your release."

Miss Sinclair sucked in a breath. "Do you always speak in such terms to a lady?"

"Only to those I wish to bed."

She yanked her arm free.

"What?" He held up his hands. "Would you prefer I lie? Besides, now we do look like lovers. Who else would quarrel in the middle of a street while people watch from their windows?"

She shook her head and strode off in front. He watched her stomp along the muddy lane. Even in the darkness, he could imagine the gentle sway of her hips hidden beneath the cape. He caught up with at the door of the inn.

"Are you coming inside?" he said. "Or would you prefer to wait out here?"

She nibbled her bottom lip. "Will there be other women in there?"

Marcus shrugged. "A few. No one will pay you the slightest attention. It's a small village. People care more about filling their coffers with coins than what's deemed proper."

"Very well," she nodded. "If I'm to play the role of mistress, I assume you've chosen a name you think fitting, something a little prettier than Ned."

He turned to face her, placed his hands on her upper arms and stared deeply into the blue twinkling gems staring back at him. "I think I'll call you Anna. After all, you are the only woman I want in my bed. Why not indulge my whimsical fantasies?"

As soon as the wooden door scraped against the tiled floor, all eyes focused on the arched entrance. All conversation came to an abrupt halt as the villagers' narrowed gazes drifted over them. Ushering Anna inside, Marcus offered Lenard a curt nod. From behind the counter, Lenard gave his usual lopsided grin in a bid to disguise the fact he had but a few teeth.

"Mr. Danbury, sir," came the immediate response from the scrawny landlord. "Give me a moment and I'll be right with you." He finished cleaning the tankard with a rag that had once been white and now looked a grimy shade of grey.

"Lenard is English?" Anna whispered.

Marcus nodded. "His wife is French."

After the crowd offered numerous nods and grumbled greetings, one by one, they turned their backs, the low muttering soon growing into a loud din.

"We'll sit over here," Marcus said, pointing to a spot near the door and in full view of Lenard.

Anna nodded, acknowledged the few people she knew and sat in the chair Marcus held out for her. "For a moment, I thought they were going to chain us to pillory and leave us for the crows to feast."

He sat forward, brushed his fingers across the soft apple of her cheek, aware of her sudden intake of breath. "Shush," he said. "You must get used to a certain level of familiarity if others are to believe our deception."

She gave a derisive snort. "In London, a gentleman does not openly court a lady. Not even his mistress."

Marcus glanced around, noting a butcher, farm labourer, the blacksmith's apprentice. "But we're not in London, Anna, we're in France. This is not high society. The people here are far more accepting. Now, would you like something to drink?"

Her cheeks flushed. "I'll have wine or ale or whatever you think is safe for consumption."

Marcus laughed as he pushed out of the chair. "I'll go up to the counter. It will give me a chance to gauge Lenard's mood without him being distracted by your beauty."

He did not give her a chance to respond and was soon back with two small pewter mugs and a copper jug half full of wine.

"Wine is easier on the stomach," Marcus said, sitting down at the table and pouring them both a drink.

Anna took a sip from the mug, shivering visibly as the potent liquid slid down her throat. "Easier on the stomach but not so on the head, I fear."

"Lenard always serves me his best."

He watched with keen interest as she took a few more sips. Was it nerves that drove her to drink more quickly? It occurred to him that they should use this time together productively. A man should delve a little deeper into a lady's mind and heart if he stood any chance of winning her favour.

"So, what will you do when you leave here?" Marcus said, relaxing back in the chair. "Will you go back to London?"

There was no chance of him doing so. Marcus vowed never to set foot on English soil again. Not while his father was alive.

Anna shrugged. "I'll never go back to London. I'm afraid I will always be regarded as Madame Labelle, proprietor of a bawdy house." She stared at the candle on the table, at the drop of wax trickling down its length. She tapped her finger to the hot liquid, rubbing it against her thumb until it solidified. "I like the country air, the lush fields and rolling hills. It brings back happy memories of my childhood."

A vision of a pretty girl with honey-gold hair flashed into his mind. He imagined her smiling, carefree, running against the wind. "How will you provide for yourself?"

In the countryside, she'd hardly find the type of work she was used to. There were no houses of ill repute desperately searching for a new madam. And there were not many men willing to take a wife with her chequered history. However, he believed her bewitching beauty was as valuable as the best debutante's dowry.

"I have a cottage nestled in a quiet country village. I have enough money put aside to give me a comfortable life."

The inquisitive, manipulative part of his brain jumped to

attention. The cottage she mentioned must surely be the same place where Miss Beaufort was hiding. It made perfect sense. Anna had fled to France while Dane's lady had fled to some quaint village to look after her cottage.

Interesting.

He was about to pry further when she said, "What of you, Marcus? Will you continue in the same vein without Tristan? I imagine you'll find working on your own far more difficult."

For some reason, it hadn't occurred to him that Tristan might not come back. A hollow void opened up in his chest, and he feigned arrogance in a bid to banish it. "I work better on my own. Tristan is too cautious, too sensible to be of any use."

Despite trying to infuse a hint of contempt into his words, he knew she did not believe his pathetic protestations. She stared into his eyes as though they were open doors to his soul. "And you're far too rash, far too reckless, which is why the two of you work so well together. I can see you'll miss him terribly."

Bloody hell.

Was she some sort of mystic? Or was he just so easy to read?

He took a large gulp of wine whilst using the opportunity to observe Lenard.

"Perhaps you judge me too harshly without knowing all the facts," he finally said, confident Lenard was simply going about his work.

She smiled and arched a brow. "I believe your scars speak volumes."

Panic flared. "Scars?" he repeated.

"There's a small one just to the left of the dimple on your chin." She pointed to the offending article. His heart thumped in his chest for an entirely different reason now. Anna had studied him sufficiently to notice his faint battle marks.

"This one came from the tip of a blade," he said, running his finger over the thin line cutting through the bristles. "Dane was with me at the time. We were ambushed whilst rescuing a lady from an asylum."

Anna's eyes widened. "Good heavens. Why were you rescuing her from an asylum?"

Marcus sighed. "It is difficult to explain. But suffice to say, the lady was not mad at all, and had been put there at the behest of her husband."

Married women were just as helpless when it came to dealing with selfish men.

"I have a few scars, too," she said, pulling up her left sleeve and turning her arm to show him her elbow. "I've one here. Can you see it?"

"This one?" He traced the pale pink line with the tip of his finger. "Is it a battle scar?"

"Yes, in a way." She yanked her sleeve back down. "I fought with Victor over a girl he brought to stay. I helped her to escape. He couldn't prove I had anything to do with it, but he still knocked me to the floor in a violent rage. I hit it on the grate."

Marcus gulped to swallow the lump in the back of his throat. If Victor were still alive, he would hunt him down and gut him like a fish.

"I'm sorry." The words tumbled from his mouth.

"Why?" She looked puzzled. "It's not your fault."

When she took a sip of wine, he nodded to her hand. "I noticed a mark on your thumb. Is it another battle scar?" Part of him did not wish to hear another tale of the cruelty she'd suffered. Part of him wanted to know every intricate detail about her.

Placing her mug back on the table, she held her hand to the candlelight. "Two gentlemen were arguing over Maudette. Sometimes men imagine the girls are in love with them. One of them threw a vase at me when I asked him to leave. I covered my head with my hands but it hit the wall next to me, and a piece grazed my thumb."

"What was his name?" His voice sounded harsh, unyielding. "The man who threw the vase."

"Why?" she laughed. "Will you sail all the way to England in a bid to avenge me?"

"No. I'll get someone else to do it on my behalf."

She stared into his eyes. "You're serious."

"I am."

Her gaze softened, and she swallowed visibly.

"I have a similar scar." He turned his hand over and showed her the mark on the pad of his palm just below his thumb. "From a woman who'd convinced herself she loved me. She charged at me with a broken perfume bottle."

She took his hand in hers and examined it beneath the flame. "You were lucky. An inch lower and it would have pierced a vein."

"An inch lower and a woman would have succeeded where many men have failed."

"Love is a dangerous business, is it not?" She gave a weak smile. "I must say I find these coincidences a little unsettling. Thank goodness I don't have scars on my back else I would be worried. I assume you received them during one of your mysterious assignments?"

A dark cloud descended, surrounding him, swallowing him whole until he almost choked on his disdain. Bitterness and resentment surfaced. He wanted to close his eyes until the feeling passed and he could breathe easy again.

"You don't need to tell me," she said, concern evident in her tone. "Forget I mentioned it."

Was he so transparent? Could she see the pain in his eyes?

"The marks have nothing to do with an assignment." He couldn't look at her, yet felt compelled to reveal his secret, to let her know why he behaved the way he did. Staring at the naked flame as it flickered back and forth, he said, "I was eighteen when my mother died at the hands of that bastard."

He stopped as raucous laughter filled the room: a response to some silly joke. Yet in his warped mind, it sounded like his father's mocking jeers.

Anna put her hand on his sleeve. "You speak of your father?"

"He is no father to me." He covered her hand with his own, the heat warming him to his core, and she did not object. "He provided the necessary funds for us to have a reasonably comfortable life. My mother was so pleased when he agreed to pay for my education. But he grew angry when I refused to visit him during the holidays, stopped paying the rent whilst I was away at school. She died in the workhouse, and I knew nothing of her plight."

He could feel his throat closing tight until he gasped for breath.

She leant forward and brushed the lock of hair from his brow. By God, he wanted to take her in his arms as a way to banish the Devil from his door.

"She died alone, Anna. I never got the chance to thank her for all she'd done for me."

A tear trickled down her cheek, and she pursed her lips, pressing them together tightly.

"When I confronted him, he had his valet hold me down while he horsewhipped me for my insolence. I have not set eyes on him since that day."

He stared into her brilliant blue eyes, taking in their radiance as though they held a magical ability to heal all pain. Out of the corner of his eye, he noticed the two men walk behind the counter and disappear through a door at the back.

Marcus exhaled, shook his head to bring his mind back to the present.

"Anna, I need you to do something for me."

"Whatever you need," she said. Her willingness to trust him caused his heart to soar.

"In a moment, I want you to shout at me, slap me hard across the face, grab your cape and march out of the door." He ignored her gasp. "Once outside, I want you to walk to your right, around to the side of the inn and wait for me there. Can you do that?"

Anna nodded though the confusion in her eyes suggested she had a thousand questions.

"You must make it look realistic," he continued. "Feel free to proceed whenever—"

The loud crack stung his skin. Even though he'd been expecting it, he almost jumped from the chair.

"Leave me alone," she cried, leaping up and throwing her cape around her shoulders.

"Anna, wait!" He called after her as she opened the door and disappeared out into the night.

Good, he thought, as numerous heads dropped as he met their curious gazes. Shrugging into his greatcoat, he threw a few coins on the table and raced out of the inn in search of his enchanting accomplice.

CHAPTER 11

Her hand stung. Her fingers throbbed where she had slapped him hard across his cheek. It had happened quickly. She'd been too scared to wait. The violent act prevented her from doing the only thing she desperately craved. It stopped her pulling him into an embrace in a bid to soothe the pain she knew festered like an open wound deep inside.

Wrapping her cape tightly around her, she turned right as instructed, stopping halfway along the outside wall of the inn to wait for him. The sound of her ragged breathing cut into the stillness of the night. Her emotions were raw, fragile, but it had nothing to do with the haunting memories of Victor.

With trembling fingers, Anna touched her chest. The wild, erratic thumping was a result of two conflicting emotions: shock and her desire for Marcus Danbury. For days, she had tried to ignore it, pushed those thoughts aside. Her feelings were harder to identify or define, having felt nothing but disdain for most men.

The obvious questions demanded her attention.

Could she trust him?

Were his amorous protestations genuine?

Or in the end, would he prove to be a worthless scoundrel?

Before she had a chance to rouse a coherent response, he charged around the side of the inn, his greatcoat flapping behind him like huge brown wings. He appeared every bit the Devil's angel: dark, brooding, a dangerous disciple on a mission to wreak havoc.

He tapped his finger to his lips as he came to stand in front of her. "We must whisper now," he said, his broad frame swamping her.

She tried to focus on the assignment. After all, it must surely be the reason behind his odd request to hit him. But his unique masculine scent filled her head, travelled through her body sparking every nerve to life.

He pressed closer. "I'll just take a look around the back of the inn."

She felt the loss instantly, her body shivering as if exposed to a bitter breeze. Why tonight? Why was she suddenly so aware of him now? Hearing his sad tale had affected her deeply.

Then he came back, standing closer still, his head just a few inches away from hers. His soft breath brushed across her cheek like a lover's caress.

Good heavens.

Was it the wine?

"The men are moving contraband from the cellar," he whispered against her ear. "There's a wooden hatch in the ground back there. We need to listen for a few minutes."

His muscular thigh brushed against her leg causing a bolt of heat to pool, her core throbbing and pulsing in response.

"How … how many men are there?"

God help her! Surely he must hear it in her voice—the overwhelming need, the deep longing.

"Two, plus Lenard."

In the darkness, she couldn't see the raised red imprint of her hand on his cheek, yet she imagined the size and the shape as a way of focusing her mind.

"Shuffle closer," he said, tugging the edge of her cape and pulling her nearer to the end of the wall.

Deep masculine whispers drifted through the air, the odd curse, a few groans, but she felt no fear.

Why would she?

She had lived with a devil for years. Nothing could ever surpass the horrors she had witnessed. Besides, she felt safe with Marcus. Just knowing he would protect her with his life caused her heart to swell.

Indeed, it proved to be the biggest revelation of all.

She had never trusted anyone. Yet despite his arrogant facade, she knew she could depend on him. Desire hit her again as she gazed up at his chiselled jaw, at the wavy locks tied at his nape, and she felt forced to clear her throat to suppress it.

"Shush," Marcus whispered.

"Did you hear something?" Lenard's voice received a mixture of replies from his devious counterparts. "Someone's out there."

"Bloody hell," Marcus cursed. "Forgive me." She was about to ask why when he pushed her back against the wall. "If you want to live don't fight me."

He claimed her mouth without any hesitation, without the teasing nips and caresses she'd expected. He didn't give her a chance to tell him she had never kissed a man. Victor had brushed her lips roughly on occasion, but nothing more.

Marcus angled his head, traced the line of her lips with his tongue and then plunged deep inside—wild and frantic. She tried to calm her breathing, tried not to choke on her inexperience. He tasted of wine, of some other potent flavour that made her head feel light and dizzy.

He tore his lips from hers, moved to nuzzle her neck and she almost sagged to the ground. "You had better start kissing me back. Else I'll be dragged off you and beaten to a pulp."

He parted her cape, his hand drifting over her hip as he claimed her mouth again. This time, she tried to clear her mind, tried to draw from the desire she felt for him. Heavens, she couldn't tell him the truth. She would have to act as though she knew what she was doing.

When his hand moved slowly up to cup her breast, things became much easier. The throbbing between her thighs returned, a frisson of excitement ran through her and so she followed his lead. Putting her hand on his hip, she tugged the shirt from his breeches, dared to let her fingers roam beneath the material, dared to let her tongue dance with his.

She sensed the shift in him immediately. The groan resonating from the back of his throat gave her more confidence to experiment. His skin felt hot to the touch, searing the tips of her fingers as they drifted over the rippled muscles in his abdomen, but his waistcoat prevented her from exploring further. Instead, she moved her hands to his nape, threaded her fingers into his hair and tugged gently.

In the distance, she heard a low chuckle, French mutterings, someone saying to leave them be, that they'd best be on their way.

She expected Marcus to pull away when she heard them slam the wooden hatch. But he continued his sensual assault, cupping her cheeks to deepen the kiss.

"God, Anna," he whispered as he stopped to catch his breath. "You make me insane with desire."

She felt her face flush, shocked at the realisation that she wanted him to kiss her again.

Without thinking, she stood on the tips of her toes and brushed her mouth softly across his. The taste of him, the earthy masculine smell that clung to his skin was like a potent elixir. The addictive essence fed her craving.

"I was expecting another slap." He raised an arrogant brow as his heated gaze lingered on her lips. "Although you seemed to be a willing participant."

"What choice did I have?" Her body still ached for his touch. "You jumped on me before I had a chance to protest."

The corners of his mouth curled up into a sinful smirk. "I have to admit I was a little surprised. I liked the way you feigned naiveté just for my benefit."

If she told him the truth, he would never believe her.

"I'm pleased you approve," she said, offering a coy smile to disguise her embarrassment. "I thought it best to add a little more authenticity to our charade."

The lie fell easily from her lips. She couldn't imagine there would be a need to kiss him again, so he need never know any different.

Without any warning, he lowered his head and kissed her once: a soft, chaste kiss on the mouth. Perhaps he had heard her thoughts and wished to protest.

"What was that for?" she asked playfully, despite feeling a frisson of fear. She wanted him to kiss her a hundred times. This strange and sudden need she had for him felt like a living thing growing inside, increasing with every touch, with every sinful look, every kind, thoughtful word.

He shrugged. "I don't know."

"Oh." She'd expected him to say it had something to do with the assignment. "What are we to do now?"

"I know what I want to do," he said as his gaze drifted over her face. "I'm just thinking of a way to pretend it's part of our plan to avoid rousing the men's suspicion."

She tapped him on the arm. "I was talking about the assignment. Are we to follow them?"

"Who?"

"Lenard's men." She couldn't help but laugh. "Are we to follow them to the cottage?"

"No. Not tonight. All I needed was confirmation Lenard is involved." He took her by the arm and led her out onto the street. "We'll go home where we can talk privately without fear of anyone overhearing, and I'll tell you my plan for tomorrow."

Anna nodded, knowing she would struggle sitting so close to him. On the journey to the inn, she'd been forced to hold her breath, to stare out into the darkness in the hope the nervous fluttering in her stomach would subside. On the journey back, whilst squashed between his muscular thighs, the same questions flooded her mind.

Why now? Why him?

Why hadn't she felt an attraction to Tristan? He was far more affable, behaved much more gentlemanly. Until a few days ago, she would have said he was more handsome.

"Tristan told me about his love for Isabella," she said, as they rode back to the monastery. He had settled his horse into a walking pace, the prolonged contact forcing her to think of a way to distract her mind. "How do you think he will fare when he sees her again?"

"Did he tell you she married Lord Fernall? Two weeks after she'd been caught eloping with him."

The contempt in his voice was unmistakable.

Anna pulled her cape tightly across her chest as the night air felt much cooler now. "There must have been a reason for it. A woman does not profess her love for one man and then marry another. Not without just cause."

He snorted. "Perhaps money and a title proved too tempting to resist."

"Trust you to be so cynical."

"I'm not cynical. I'm just a little distrustful of people and their motives."

She knew why. The trauma of losing his mother under such circumstances was the cause of all his negative character traits.

"Perhaps Isabella found herself in a difficult situation," she said with a sigh.

"She had a home, Anna, people to care for her. What possible reason could there have been to induce her to marry a man she didn't love?"

She glanced up, noting his stern expression. "Things aren't always so simple." Her own experiences caused a mixture of sadness and regret to infuse her tone.

What possible reason could *she* have had for choosing to live in a brothel? But there had been no choice. She'd had no one to care for her, and consequently, there had been no one to question her failure to return home from the Servants' Registry Office.

An icy shiver ran all the way down to her toes as she remembered the elation burning in her chest at being offered the position of a governess in the home of a French comte.

"You may lean in closer if you're cold," Marcus said, teasing the horse into a canter. "We'll be home in a few minutes."

The word *home* roused a mixture of emotions.

Home had been a small country hamlet—a place where love blossomed, where happiness and contentment were part of everyday life. Since meeting the comte, home had become a distant, painful memory.

The hulking black shadow of the monastery loomed into view. For some unknown reason, the place had begun to feel like home. Being safe and living without fear had brought about a change in her. Never before had she contemplated her own needs and desires.

The time spent out in the garth had given her an appreciation for the simple pleasures of life. In the chapel, she had found a way to soothe the pain of the past. Spending time in Marcus Danbury's company had awakened a deep need in her—a sense of longing she had never thought to experience.

Her heart was akin to a bird recovering from a broken wing. The first flutter felt strange, still painful. She fought against it, frightened to acknowledge the fact it might never fully heal, that she would always be a little less than whole. But the more desire flowed through her, the more her heart soared, the stronger she became.

She glanced up at the gentleman responsible for these new sensations, unable to suppress a shiver as their gazes locked.

"We're home now," he said, and she felt a pang of regret. When the time came, she would have no choice but to leave this idyllic place.

She would have no choice but to leave the only man she had ever truly desired.

CHAPTER 12

"I look ridiculous," Anna grumbled as she smoothed her hands down the front of a pair of Tristan's old breeches. "I'm not wearing them. Heavens, if Victor were alive he would shoot me where I'm standing."

"But he's not alive, so you may do as you please. They look fine to me."

Marcus lounged back in the chair behind his desk, folded his arms across his chest and considered her attire. The breeches were far too baggy around the knees though he was more preoccupied with the way they hugged the lush curve of her hips. He had noticed her shapely ankles the moment she had walked in and so perhaps was somewhat biased.

"Well, they don't feel fine," she huffed.

"Turn around and let me look at them." Curiosity and the thrum of desire forced him to be bold, yet he tried to maintain a neutral tone. In her naiveté, she turned, threw her hands in the air in frustration and offered him the most delightful view. "Is it that they're too tight?" he asked, although, in his expert opinion, they enhanced the soft round cheeks to perfection.

"Perhaps it's the pale material," she complained. "But I feel as though my legs are bare."

A vision of her creamy limbs flashed into his mind. They were long, extremely flexible, the fleshy part of her inner thighs like plump pillows made to cushion his muscular limbs as he thrust hard inside her.

Damn it all. After tasting her lips, he'd thought of nothing else all night.

"I'll say it again. I think they look perfectly respectable." His voice sounded strained, an octave or two higher. "Perfectly suitable for what we've got planned."

She shook her head defiantly as she swung back round to face him. "No. I'm changing."

He almost groaned, dropped to his knees and begged her to reconsider. "You must do what you feel is best. But know we will be walking half a mile or more through the woods in the dark. We may even venture down to the shore. There's a cave I wish to examine which means we will be climbing a few rocks."

If that wasn't enough to convince her, he didn't know what would.

"I'll be fine." She shrugged. "I'll lose the petticoat and stays, wear sturdy boots."

Heaven help him.

The woman knew exactly what to say to torment and tease. Had there been monks still living in the monastery he had no doubt they'd fall prey to her feigned innocence as a means of seduction.

Marcus swallowed. "Won't you be cold?" he asked, knowing she would only have to say the word, and he would soon warm her body.

"Not during such vigorous activity."

Was she deliberately trying to provoke a reaction?

"A good walk through the woods does wonders to get the blood pumping," she added.

His blood seemed to pump only in one direction, pooling in

the only part of his anatomy that mattered.

"I shall ready the horses while you change." If he didn't put some distance between them, he would do something foolish, something he might regret.

He opened the desk drawer, removed his leather-bound notebook and pencil. Dudley Spencer's most recent letter caught his attention. He had written again requesting information regarding Miss Beaufort's whereabouts and would not cease until satisfied. The gentleman was nothing if not persistent, and Marcus did not care to be reminded of the debt he owed them.

"Horses? Are we not riding together?"

Marcus could not decide if her tone held a hint of relief or disappointment. "I need to know you're free to leave if I am intercepted during our investigation."

She raised her chin, made no comment as to the inconsistency of his argument compared to the previous night, and simply said, "Oh."

He stood, the throbbing bulge in his breeches had eased somewhat. His need to uncover the information Dudley required being enough to dampen his ardour.

As she opened the door to leave, she stopped and glanced over her shoulder. "Just so we're clear. Despite what occurs this evening. I would not leave you under any circumstances."

The words hit him like a hard punch to the jaw. Similar words had left his lips once, spoken to the mother who had given her love so freely. He nodded as he could not form a response. Closing his eyes briefly, he exhaled slowly as she left the room and closed the door behind her. Anna Sinclair affected him like no other woman before. Her loyalty knew no bounds. It was a rare quality, something he knew he should treasure.

The cracking and crunching underfoot was loud enough to rouse an army of men from their slumber. "Can you not be a little lighter in your steps?" he whispered as he led the way through the woods. "It doesn't matter now. But as we get closer, I don't want to alert them to our presence."

"You were right," she muttered. "I should have worn those blasted breeches." Her curse revealed the depth of her frustration. "I keep snagging my dress and can barely see where to place my feet."

Marcus smiled, thankful she could not see his amused expression in the dark. "I did warn you. Here, take my hand if it's easier."

"It's so dark. How do you know which way to go?"

"I have walked these woods a hundred times or more."

He stopped and offered his hand. Their gazes locked for a moment and she took it without hesitation. With neither of them wearing gloves, her hot palm kindled the flaming passion simmering inside. Indeed, now that he'd tasted her lips he doubted anything could extinguish it.

"Let's hope there are no horse thieves wandering about." She sighed as she glanced back over her shoulder. "Are you sure it was wise to leave them tied to the tree?"

She really did baffle him. Sometimes he believed she had the strength and resolve of the strongest of men. As Madame Labelle, she knew how to convey a certain power and level of independence. He had heard it in her tone numerous times. Yet there was an air of innocence about her whenever she expressed her worries and fears. He liked both aspects of her character.

Both made his cock stir.

"The horses will be safe." He tightened his grip on her hand, the need to comfort and protect pushing to the fore. "We'll need to remain silent for a moment as the cottage is in a clearing just beyond these trees."

"Wait," she whispered, tugging on his hand. "Remind me what we're doing here."

Marcus turned to face her. Golden strands of hair framed her face beneath the dark hood of her cape. Turquoise-blue eyes stared back at him, and he resisted the urge to claim her mouth.

"I need to know for certain what they intend to smuggle. I'll make a note of it so I can track when it's being moved."

She nodded.

"You can wait here for me," he added. "I'll be five minutes at most."

"No. You said you needed my help. If we're spotted, we will pretend to be lovers."

Perhaps it was time he accepted the truth of it.

He did not really need her with him and despite her concern over the comte's accomplice, he was sure she'd be safe inside the monastery. But for some strange reason he wanted an excuse to be close to her. Yes, if the men suspected they were lovers, it did provide a plausible reason to be out alone at night. Indeed, he had grown tired of pretending. He could make it happen. It would not take much to rouse her desire.

"Very well. Stay close. And don't be surprised if I need to kiss you again."

The stone cottage had been abandoned for years. Had it been on Marcus' land, he would have repaired the roof, fixed the windows, and used it as a cosy hunting cabin. The absence of any light spilling out from the windows did not mean the place lay empty.

They watched and waited for a few minutes. He tried to focus on the assignment but the lady at his side still gripped his hand, and he could feel the warmth of her body radiate through his palm.

If he had timed things correctly, the men should be at the inn collecting all the contraband they could carry. But it paid to be cautious. Tapping his finger to his lips to secure her silence, they crept towards the north wall. With one of the frames missing from the window, it afforded an opportunity to peer inside.

It took a moment for his eyes to grow accustomed to the darkness, to realise the tall black shadows were nothing more than items of furniture. The deafening silence convinced him no one was home.

"We'll take a look inside," he mouthed, his voice quieter than a whisper.

With some hesitation he opened the door, the damp, swollen wood catching on the floor to restrict their access.

"If we force it, they'll know someone's been here."

They squeezed through the gap, coming to stand next to the table. A thick layer of dust, dead flies and leaves littered the surface. A lantern, an empty bottle and various food-encrusted utensils sat amongst the debris.

"Are you sure they came here?" she asked, standing so close her arm brushed against his, forcing him to swallow down his desire for her again.

He scanned the room. "I followed them here a few nights ago. Damn it all. They can't have moved the goods already." If Coombes failed to catch them, he would refuse to give Marcus another assignment. "Come."

They moved through the dilapidated house, glancing up at the exposed wooden beams where parts of the ceiling had fallen away, stepping carefully to avoid the broken boards.

"There's nothing here," she whispered. "They must have been back and moved it all."

"If they have, they'll have moved the stash closer to the shore. I can guarantee they'll be heading out in a day or two."

"What were you expecting to find here?"

He shrugged. "Tobacco, brandy, maybe tea or bolts of fabric. I'll look around once more and then we'll head to the cave. Perhaps they've moved it down there."

Anna nodded and followed him around the cottage while he tapped the boards with his heel, searched cupboards, looked under the bed.

"I know you have a job to do," she began as he closed the cottage door. "But have you considered the fact that these men have no choice but to behave as they do?"

Marcus scoffed as he took her hand again and led her back through the woods. "If you're going to regale sorrowful tales of soldiers forced to smuggle to feed their families now the war's over, I've heard it all before."

"Don't you feel a little compassion for them? They fought for their country only to be discarded when it was all over."

"I feel for anyone who struggles to feed their children, but I draw the line at those who threaten the innocent. Those who would kill to make a few guineas."

"Have you always done this sort of work?" she asked, and he noticed she sounded a little breathless in her bid to keep up with his long strides.

"In one form or another." He would have sold his soul to the Devil rather than accept funds from his father.

She tightened her grip as they climbed through the undergrowth, stepping out onto an overgrown path. "What will happen to them, to the smugglers?"

Marcus shrugged. "It's likely the revenue ship will intercept them at sea. If not, there are numerous watchhouses dotted along the coast. My contact will inform the Custom House. They will decide how to proceed."

He could feel her intense gaze on his face. "Do you do this for the money, for your country?"

"I do it to survive. For no other reason than that."

They exited the woods through a clearing. The crescent moon's reflection cast a shimmering path across the inky expanse of water. The cliff edge stood no more than a hundred feet away.

Anna inhaled deeply. "It's beautiful here. I could spend hours gazing out at the view." She turned to face him, the wind whipping the tendrils of hair escaping from her hood. "Is it easy to get down to the shore?"

"There's a path to the right," he said, pointing out into the darkness. "It leads down to a sandy beach. The tide is high but drops by five feet or so every hour. We'll have to climb over the rocks to access the cave, but there's no danger of it flooding." He glanced down at her dress. "Do you think you'll be able to manage it? You can sit and wait for me here if you wish. I don't think Lenard's men will venture out when the tide is at its peak."

"No. I'll come with you. If you're wrong, we'll have a better chance of explaining why we're out here if we're together."

"You mean we can put our 'lovers desperate to sate their desire' plan to work?"

She cast him a coy smile. "Yes, if faced with no other choice."

God, it was almost worth stumbling upon the smugglers just for an excuse to taste her again.

The three-foot drop from the cliff edge to the rocks below posed no problem for a man wearing boots and breeches. Anna had been forced to sit on the grassy verge and shuffle down into his arms. It took all the strength he had to keep his balance on the slippery stones. The delectable lady in his arms clung to his shoulders, trying desperately not to fall as the spray from the crashing waves covered the surface.

"Next time, perhaps you will listen to me when I tell you to wear the breeches." He took her hand as she jumped from the last rock to the sandy bed at the cave's entrance.

"Next time? Hopefully, we won't need to come here again." She brushed the dirt from her cape. "But I concede. You were right. I should have listened."

It took a strong woman to admit defeat.

"Stay close. Perhaps it would be better if you held on to me as it will be nigh on impossible to see anything in the cave. I'll have to wait until we're some way inside before I can light the candle. There could be a lugger waiting off the coast and someone might mistake it for a signal."

Anna took his right arm, and he used his left hand to guide them around the perimeter. The moisture in the air made every surface feel wet and damp. With numerous rocks and shale underfoot, they had to be careful where they placed their feet.

"Could we not have come here during the day?" she complained.

"I can't take the chance of being seen. Not when my assignment is so close to home. The villagers would never trust me again if they knew of my involvement."

"That's why I don't understand why you agreed to do it."

"I don't get to pick and choose which assignments I take, Anna." His tone sounded blunt as a way to mask feeling guilt for his deceit. "Someone alerted Coombes of the plan to smuggle goods from here, and he instructed me to investigate."

"Isn't there a better way for you to earn a living?"

"I can't believe you're giving me advice in that regard."

She ignored his comment. "Who owns the land to the north of the monastery? You could farm—ow!"

Marcus grabbed her arm as she stumbled. "Are you all right?"

"Yes, yes." She sounded breathless, and he silently cursed for bringing her into the cave under such perilous conditions. "I'm fine."

"Perhaps we should leave, come back when—wait, there's something over here."

The toe of his boot hit a solid object, the thud alerting him to the chest. "Let go of my arm for a moment. I need to reach into my bag."

She obeyed his request, and he rummaged around in the leather satchel draped over his shoulder until he found what he was searching for. In the damp atmosphere, it took a minute or so to strike a light with the tinderbox.

"Hold this," he said, handing her the candle. "I need to see what's inside the chest."

He raised the lid, the sound of creaking hinges echoing through the cavern, to find tea and tobacco stored inside custom-made linen bags to be worn underneath clothing. There were reams of silk thread and behind the chest he found four half ankers, each one capable of holding four gallons of spirits.

After making a note of all the items, he closed the lid.

"What will you do now?" Anna asked. He could hear the nervous edge in her tone coupled with a hint of excitement. The thrill accompanying their discovery had heightened his awareness and despite the salty air, the sweet smell of almonds flooded his senses.

"I'll send a message detailing the goods. Explain that they'll be leaving in a day or two." He glanced at Anna. The soft glow from the candle illuminated her face. He'd never met a woman whose inner beauty radiated brighter than any superficial charm. "We should leave."

He took her hand, intending to lead her back to the entrance. But now he had achieved his goal, his desire for her flamed anew.

"Why? Do you expect the men to return?"

"No." He turned to face her, stroked her cheek with the back of his fingers. She made no objection. The candle in her hand quivered, the flickering flame revealing a nervous edge. "Although, wait—" He stopped abruptly and scanned the cave. "I … I thought I heard something."

Her frantic gaze flew to the entrance, and he waited for her to turn to face him before blowing out the candle.

"What … what shall we do?" she panted.

"The only thing we can do." In the dark, he hoped she could not see his sinful grin. "Pretend to be lovers," he said as he pulled her closer and claimed her tempting lips.

CHAPTER 13

Anna could tell from his rich, seductive tone what he intended to do. Still, she'd had no time to protest, no time to plan how best to proceed. Not that she wanted to protest. She had thought of nothing other than his soft lips all night.

Marcus Danbury oozed masculine charm. The earthy scent of his skin, the way his lips curved into a seductive smile, and his strong muscular thighs, all posed an intoxicating combination. She wondered if she felt the potent thrum of passion more strongly because she had never desired a man before. Now, she understood what kept the randy lords of the *ton* up all night.

"I want you so badly." He practically growled the words as he sucked in a breath and pressed her back against the stone wall.

She panted, but excitement and anticipation prevented her from forming a single word.

As Marcus' mouth ravaged hers again, all rational thought left her. Lenard's men were not about to pounce on them.

They were alone in an isolated cave.

They were alone in the dark.

The warmth of his mouth inflamed her body. There was

nothing slow or measured about the way he kissed her. Like a true pirate, he took what he wanted, plundering hard and deep with his tongue until she clutched at his shoulders.

In the cave, it was cold and damp, but the heat from the hard body pressed against her penetrated the thin layers of clothing. While his mouth moved over hers, his hands were everywhere—frantic, desperate touches that left the hairs at her nape tingling.

"Holy hell," he groaned as his hands settled on her buttocks to draw her against the evidence of his arousal. "I've never wanted anyone as much as I want you." Desire shot through her as he rained kisses down her neck. "Tell me you want me, too."

"I do." The words tumbled from her lips. She felt dizzy, her head so light and free. A deep, clawing need settled between her thighs, the beating pulse growing in intensity.

He must have sensed her desperation as his hand drifted up her bare leg, his fingers rubbing against her most sensitive spot.

"Forget everything I said about wearing breeches," he panted, stroking her back and forth until she gasped for breath. "I was wrong."

"Marcus … wait … I …"

In the dark, all other senses were heightened. His musky scent filled her head. His hot, wet tongue stimulated every fibre of her being as it danced and tangled with hers. She could feel a pleasurable tension building within. A desperate ache. Each motion of his fingers brought her closer to the place where she would cry out his name.

"Don't stop," she gasped.

"I don't intend to. But let me hear your thoughts. Tell me how it feels for me to touch you."

He kept up the rhythmical motion until her body tingled, until the muscles in her core gave way to faint, sporadic contractions.

"It feels divine," she whispered as he had taken her far beyond the need for modesty.

"Tell me how close you are. Tell me you want to feel me move inside you."

"Yes," she said, not really understanding his intention. She felt his fingers penetrate her, the muscles hugging them as though they were the answer to her prayers.

"You're ready for me," he said with a low hum. "Do you want me, Anna?"

"Yes." She had never wanted anything more in her entire life.

He fumbled around with his breeches, pushed his hands up under her dress to grasp her bare buttocks as he lifted her. "Wrap your legs around me, your arms about my neck."

She did as he asked, desire raging through her veins. She felt him then, pushing inside her, thick and solid. Swallowing a gulp, it suddenly occurred to her to tell him the truth.

"Wait," she panted, her breathless word lost amidst the sound of crashing surf echoing through the cave. "Marcus."

"God, you're so sweet, Anna."

When she opened her mouth to caution him, he claimed it again, delved deeper with his tongue as he thrust inside her with a loud groan of appreciation.

Her throat muscles spasmed, but she managed to let out a painful cry. "No. Please, wait." Every muscle in her body felt stiff, rigid. The pain was short, sharp, quickly subsiding. "Give me a minute," she gasped. "I've not done this before."

"I know it's a little cold, but we'll soon warm up."

"I … I've never been with a man," she managed to say as he thrust inside her again.

Marcus froze.

"Bloody hell," he muttered as she felt him withdraw. "What the hell do you mean?" He lowered her down until her feet touched the carpet of sand and shale. "Damn it, where's the bloody candle?"

"I dropped it."

He fiddled with his breeches, then stepped closer until she could see the amber flecks in his brown eyes, could feel his breath against her cheek. “Tell me I imagined it. Tell me I am so drunk with desire I misheard you.”

“No, no. There’s no mistake.” The guilt in her voice was evident.

“Why the hell didn’t you tell me?”

“I should have said something sooner.”

“A damn sight sooner.” His anger was replaced with a frustrated sigh. “Please tell me how you can spend years working in a blasted brothel and still be a virgin?”

His question caused memories of Victor to surface.

“Victor was a complicated man, obsessed with propriety. I doubt you would have believed me even if I had told you the truth.”

Why did she sound so weak and pathetic? Why did she feel so inadequate?

“Probably,” he said honestly. “I’m struggling to believe it now.”

Desire still thrummed through her veins. Her heart pumped rapidly and tiny beads of perspiration formed on her brow. Where was Marie Labelle when she needed her?

“Well, I’m sorry if the whole thing has been a huge disappointment.” She batted at her dress, pulled up the hood of her cape, and squared her shoulders. “I’m certain virgins lack the skill necessary to please your licentious needs.”

“Why are you so angry?” He brushed the strands of hair from her face.

Anna shrugged. Perhaps she liked the way he looked at her when he assumed she had the experience to please him? Perhaps embarrassment had forced her to be blunt. Yet she suspected her feelings stemmed from a deep sadness, regret for having not had the opportunity to be close to him.

“Why are *you* so angry?” she countered.

He exhaled loudly and shook his head. "Probably because I have never taken a woman's virginity and never had any intention of doing so. It complicates things."

Well, she could not berate him for his lack of honesty.

"I should have told you," she reiterated. "I just … I didn't expect things to progress so quickly."

"So quickly?" He chuckled. "I've been waiting all day to feel your lips on mine again." He took her chin between his finger and thumb, not as firmly as Victor used to do, but he mistook her shiver for something else. "Look. You're cold, and we need to get back to the monastery. But I need to know, Anna. I need to know if you still want me."

She could feel her cheeks suddenly burn. "I do," she said, swallowing down her nerves.

He gave a relieved sigh. "Then on the way home you can tell me how you managed to save yourself, how you kept such a treasured prize in a world full of debauched heathens."

"It wasn't a choice, Marcus. You should know that if Victor had wanted me, I would have been powerless to prevent it."

He muttered a curse. "Then I am grateful the man was a hypocrite and a fool. Indeed, I am grateful he is dead. It saves me the trouble of running a blade through his black heart."

She gave a weak smile, touched her fingers to his cheek. "If only you had been there to save me all those years ago."

He turned his head and kissed the tips of her fingers. "But I am here for you now."

The shock following his surprising discovery still resonated deep within.

Damn it all.

If he'd have known she was a virgin he would have—what? Refused to press his attention upon her? Been cold for fear she might do something as ridiculous as fall in love with him? Isn't that what virgins were known to do—profess undying love to the first man to tickle their fancy?

Although in truth, he was the one who felt changed by the experience. Perhaps the ache in his chest came from a burning desire to mate with her? Was that why her welcoming body had felt so magnificent? Was that why he had an overwhelming desire to take her to his chamber and never let her leave?

Marcus mentally shook his head and focused on the conversation. "How old were you when your parents died?" He took her hand again as he guided her back through the woods.

"Twenty. I suppose I could have stayed in Marlow, married a local man—"

"You had offers?" He was not surprised. What man wouldn't want a wife so beautiful it made his cock ache just looking at her?

"I received an offer or two. But I was naive enough to believe in love. I refused to settle for anything less." She sighed. "And so I went to London with the intention of working for a year or so."

Marcus cupped her elbow as they navigated the bank. Once they were safely on the path, he let go. "So you took employment with the comte?"

"It was my fault. I should have only accepted work through the Registry Office. But when a French comte approached me dressed in all his finery, I was seduced by the idea of working in a grand house."

Marcus snorted. "You wouldn't be the first woman to fall for such a trick. When did you realise you'd made a mistake?"

"On the first night." She paused, and he wondered if the memory caused her pain. "He locked me in the bedchamber and kept me there for weeks. After he had explained why he'd hired me, I had no option but to accept the position."

It still didn't explain how she'd kept her virginity.

"Did he have some sort of sight impairment?"

She looked at him and frowned. "Why would you think that?"

"There must be something wrong with him if he kept you as mistress of his brothel but never … well."

"Victor believed a mother must be virtuous. He wanted someone to mother the girls, oversee his business without being tempted by debauchery and sin. It seems, to my detriment, I have the deportment of a duchess and the manners of a marchioness. It sounds pathetic, I know, but he despised weak men. He would not taint our relationship with such a personal act, yet he was often prone to violent outbursts, erratic behaviour."

"Then the irony is he was just as weak as those he despised."

"The constant threat of violence causes emotional debilitation. I was forever looking over my shoulder wondering if the breath I had just taken would be my last. To live like that takes its toll."

Marcus gripped her hand, stroked it with his thumb. "Does Dane know all of this?"

"Of course not. I've never told a soul, not even Miss Beaufort."

The mere mention of the woman's name caused a pang of dread. Dudley wanted answers, and he would harangue Marcus until he got the information he needed. Anna had mentioned the village of Marlow. It was forty or so miles from London, an easy journey for a woman to travel to on her own.

"And so, in killing Victor, you have inadvertently been left with no form of income and no abode."

"Not at all. Victor was shrewd in his business dealings, and I learnt to do the same. It took a few years, but I managed to save enough money to buy the small cottage I told you about. The lords of London can be generous if you accommodate their needs." Her tone revealed a level of pride in her achievements.

"I could never have left him whilst he was still alive. But I always hoped that one day I would go home."

Damn it.

Marcus wanted to punch the air in frustration. He wished he could erase her last comment from his memory, pretend his poor analytical skills made it impossible for him to piece together the relevant bits of information.

"And you killed him because you had no choice." Discussing Victor was a way of focusing his mind on something other than Anna's cottage in Marlow.

They came to the tree where he'd tied the horses. Both animals stood patiently waiting for their return.

"Victor tried to shoot me, but his man sacrificed his life to save me." She stroked her horse, gave it a reassuring pat. "He was about to shoot Lord Danesfield when I stabbed him in the back. He would have killed me, too."

The gravity of her words rendered him mute.

He was tired of talking about the past. Imagining her in such a terrifying predicament caused his blood to boil. The need to protect her was fierce. He wondered if it had anything to do with the feeling of helplessness he experienced over his mother's death. Indeed, it was the reason he shied away from emotional entanglements.

When she gripped the reins, he said, "Here, let me help you up." Like the best groom, he talked her through keeping the saddle straight, guided her foot into the stirrup.

"Thank you." She offered a weak smile. "I'm not used to riding."

He mounted his horse, and they rode back towards the monastery at a slow pace, the mood somewhat subdued when compared to the frenzy of activity experienced in the cave. The thought brought the memory flooding back: their urgent hands, the groans and pants. His desire for her still simmered beneath the surface, accompanied by a gut-wrenching feeling of guilt for deflowering a virgin against a cold, damp wall.

"In my frustration, I failed to apologise for the rather unrefined way I went about things." After all she had been through, she deserved so much better.

"It doesn't matter," she said with a sigh. "Let's forget about it, put it behind us. Perhaps some things are not destined to be."

Panic flared. What the hell was she saying? The thought of not having her in his bed caused his heart to beat rapidly.

"I wouldn't say that. One little setback hardly constitutes failure." He was beginning to sound desperate.

"Madame Labelle would have been stronger. She would not have allowed it to happen."

"But she's not here." He turned and met her weary gaze. "Besides, during the years spent in the brothel, you were merely playing a role. Anna Sinclair is the woman I have come to know." The woman I have come to admire and respect, he added silently. "And I believe she wanted it to happen just as much as I did."

Her gaze drifted over his face, ventured down the length of his body. "But we acted in the moment." Good. She had not denied she wanted him. "I doubt it would be the same again."

It took a tremendous amount of effort not to chuckle. She really was naive when it came to amorous liaisons. He would wager everything he owned he could rouse her desire within minutes, maybe seconds.

"Well, call me chivalrous, but I feel it only courteous to try to make amends for my lack of attentiveness."

A smile touched her lips. "I would not wish to deny you the opportunity to display your gallantry. But don't you have a letter to write?"

For a moment he imagined she was talking about his letter to Dudley. The letter where he would betray the trust she'd placed in him. But then it occurred to him she meant his letter alerting

Coombes of the smugglers impending departure. Never in all his working years or during all of his assignments had he placed his own needs before those relating to his duty.

"The letter can wait," he said. His desire for Anna Sinclair was the only thing that mattered to him.

To atone for his uncouth behaviour, he would give her a night to remember.

CHAPTER 14

With the passing of each new day, Marie Labelle faded away into the background. Anna found she was not as cynical as her alter ego: the character she had hidden behind as a way of coping with the pain and sorrow. Indeed, she had grown to trust Marcus Danbury. Somehow, he had managed to find his way through the solid ice cavity and into her heart.

Reconnecting with the spirited, innocent girl she had once been caused a wealth of emotions to push forth: excitement, hope, and desire. The deep sense of longing was a new feeling, one neither Marie nor Anna had experienced before. Consequently, numerous attempts to define it had left her baffled.

"We'll have to tend to the horses." Marcus' rich voice broke her reverie. He helped her down, holding her close to his body until her feet settled firmly on the ground. Desire sparked anew. "Help me remove the tack and brush them down. After the slow ride back there'll be no need to walk them to cool their muscles."

Her body thrummed with anticipation.

After their chores, would he suggest another shared activity? Such a mundane job as brushing down the horses should have left her feeling cold. But there was something seductive about the way he went about the task. During each long, soothing stroke his eyes flashed with hot sensuality as he failed to look at anything else but her.

"What now?" she said as they settled the animals into the stable.

"Now we must attend to the needs of the riders. And I intend to give a lot more time and attention to the task."

She laughed as they crossed the courtyard heading for the monastery's oak door, the sound a way of expelling the hot air filling her lungs, a way of cooling her heated blood. "What? Are we to brush each other down, relax our muscles, and take something refreshing to drink?"

"Yes, in a manner of speaking." He closed the door behind them, pulling down the heavy bar to offer added security. "I suggest you let me take the lead. I am somewhat adept when it comes to doing a thorough job."

"Is that why you were so angry with me in the cave?"

"Had you explained your situation, I would have done things a little differently, yes."

Anna threaded her arm through his as they walked through the nave. The echo of his boots on the tiled floor cut through the silence. "I assume the servants are all in their beds?"

"More than likely. They're used to my unconventional habits. Sometimes, Andre waits until I'm home." She let go of his arm as he opened the door to the chapter house. The room was dark, and he removed his coat, lifted the strap of his leather bag over his head and placed both items on the chair. "Would you like something to drink?"

"What do you have?"

"Definitely brandy. I always keep a flask in the drawer unless Tristan has downed the lot." He moved to the small round table in the corner, picked up a bottle and shook it. "You're in luck. There's port, too."

"I'll have a drop of port."

When he sauntered over to give her the glass, a sinful smile touched his lips. A sensual aura emanated from every fibre of his being. The seductive energy soothed her aching muscles, brought a level of inner calm despite the fact her heart thumped wildly in her chest.

"We'll drink it here and then head upstairs, so I'll not bother to light the lamp." He stared at her over the rim of his glass as he sipped his port.

It was as though she had forgotten how to perform simple tasks such as breathing and swallowing and almost dribbled the burgundy liquid down her cape and dress when her mouth refused to comply.

As Marcus watched her use her finger to wipe the residue from her chin, he stepped forward. "Allow me."

She expected him to produce a small piece of linen, but to her surprise, he held her finger to his lips and sucked the tip softly. His mouth was warm, wet, utterly wicked. The sensation caused sparks of desire to ignite. Like a blacksmith's furnace, the fire inside raged fast and furious, melting away any doubts and reservations. As the master of the flame, he could bend and mould her easily to his will. Just as she had done in the cave, she would give herself over to him, right now if he wished it so.

Her gazed drifted over the breadth of his chest, ventured to the desk behind him.

His tongue circled the tip of her finger before he pulled it slowly out of his mouth. "Don't get any ideas. We're not staying here." Even his silky smooth tone sent ripples of excitement racing through her, the pulse between her thighs beating a powerful, pleasurable rhythm.

"Do you presume to know my thoughts?" she said, unable to keep her desire for him from infusing her tone.

"You cannot glance at the desk with that sultry smile and not expect me to draw my own conclusions." He nodded to her glass. "Drink up, for the anticipation is killing me."

Now she wished she had asked for a much larger measure. Not because she wished to stall him. But she needed a way to bolster her courage. With a slight tremble in her fingers, she swallowed what remained in her glass. Marcus took it from her and placed it on the desk behind him.

"Come." He took her hand. "Let's find somewhere more comfortable."

"Are we going to my chamber or … or yours?" she said in a bid to sound more confident.

"Mine."

How could one simple, solitary word cause a shiver to race through her body? No doubt his masterful tone played some part in rousing such a reaction.

They climbed the stairs in silence though her internal voice refused to be tempered. Question after question flooded her mind. Would her disdain for the patrons of Labelles, for the debauched scenes she'd so frequently witnessed, prevent her from enjoying the experience? Would she know how to please him or would she fall hopelessly short of his expectations? What would happen when the time came for her to leave the monastery and return to England?

The last thought caused a frisson of fear, and she quickly pushed it aside so as not to ruin the moment.

His quarters were at the end of the long corridor, the furthest room from her own, she noted, and she recalled his reserved, austere facade when he'd first shown her up to her chamber.

"Please, come in," he said, as she hugged the door jamb like one would a mast on a sinking ship. With some hesitation, Anna stepped over the threshold and into his private domain. "Give me a moment. I'll just light the candle lamps."

She stood in the middle of the vast space. Where her room was small and cosy, his was three times larger, maybe more. As a soft, warm glow illuminated the shadows, she scanned her surroundings, believing his choice of decor would reveal much of his character.

"What's happened to your bed?" she asked, surprised to find it stood no more than a few inches from the floor. For a man with such a large frame, it could hardly be comfortable.

Marcus glanced at it and shrugged. "I built it myself. It's just a frame without legs. I've spent years sleeping in barns, on the ground, anywhere I could lay my head. I sleep better the lower I am to the floor."

"Oh," she replied, noting how the room had an inherently masculine feel. All the soft furnishings, from the drapes to the coverlet, were in varying shades of green. There was something natural about it, something unassuming, earthy.

"It's far more comfortable than it looks," he said as he strode past her. She heard him close the door and turn the key in the lock. "Now, do you wish to go first or second?"

She swung around to face him. "Excuse me?" Confusion caused her to frown. But her breath caught in her throat as he stepped closer and tugged the ties at her neck, pushed her cape off her shoulders. "How … what …?"

Marcus took her hand, forcing her to step out from the pool of material. "We'll spend a little time getting to know one another." His heated gaze roamed over her dress. "Thankfully, your decision to forgo a few layers has made my work a lot easier."

She had no idea what he meant. No idea what he intended to do. It had all been very simple, all been very base at Labelles. Copulation amounted to nothing more than lots of heaving, grunts and banging. The girls feigned desire. They were desperate to be rid of their partners. Even the erotic paintings lining the wall in the drawing room had failed to provide the enlightenment needed to respond to Marcus' odd question.

Anna shook her head, honesty being her only option. "I haven't the faintest idea what you mean."

He stared at her for a moment; an arrogant grin played at the corners of his mouth, and she felt her cheeks burn. "Then I shall gladly go first." He led her to the edge of the bed. "Wait here."

Anna watched him fill the wash bowl from the pitcher, throw a few sprigs of dried lavender into the water along with a linen square.

Coming back to stand in front of her, he flexed his fingers. "I'm going to undress you, unless you've changed your mind."

"No. I've not changed my mind." Heavens, she had spent years feeling nothing but disdain. She welcomed the multitude of pleasurable emotions coursing through her.

Marcus smiled. Placing his hands on her shoulders, he turned her around, began slowly undoing the row of buttons on her dress. Her breath came quick; her head felt light at the touch of his nimble fingers as they traced a line down the length of her back. The garment slithered to the floor. She shivered visibly when he gathered her chemise and pulled it over her head to leave him with a clear view of her naked behind.

He sucked in a breath. "Lord help me, restraint is going to be far more difficult than I thought."

She couldn't speak. She could feel him standing close, almost jumped when he rained featherlight kisses along her shoulder. With her eyes closed, her body reacted to every touch, to every breath that drifted over her skin. She knew the moment he moved away.

"Don't turn around. Not yet." His tone was rich and heavy amidst the sound of splashing water. "It might feel cold at first."

As soon as the soaked linen touched her skin, she inhaled sharply, arching her back to pull away. "Good Lord."

"Hush," he whispered, pressing his mouth against her ear as one hand settled on her hip while the other wiped over her back with the damp cloth. A hint of lavender drifted through the air to tease her senses. "Your skin is so soft." The hand at her hip moved in caressing circles.

"It … it doesn't feel as cold now." She felt dizzy, drunk, a little disorientated as she swayed with his soothing touch. A bolt of desire shot to her core when he wiped the cool, moist piece of linen over her buttocks. "Marcus," came her breathless pant.

He must have dropped the cloth because two strong hands gripped her hips. Falling to his knees, he kissed along the base of her spine, moved lower to nip and lick each bare cheek.

The heavy feeling between her legs grew in intensity.

"Tell me you want me to touch you," he said. "Tell me you want to feel my hands all over your body."

"I do," she panted, a moan falling from her lips as he stroked the outside of her thigh, moving up the inside to skim lightly over the place that ached for him. "I do." Her tone revealed her impatience.

"Tell me what you want, Anna."

"Touch me," she whispered, feeling no shame. "Touch me again."

"Like this?" His fingers travelled up her thigh, brushed against her sex, and she groaned as she moved against them.

"Yes."

Her breasts felt full and heavy, the slight chill in the air causing her nipples to peak. Desire raged through her like nothing she had ever felt before. The need to feel close to him, to feel him cover her body, push deep into her core, was overwhelming.

She almost whimpered when he dropped his hand, but the rustling of garments, the thud of boots hitting the floor convinced her he would soon be naked, too. With her heart beating so loudly, she gasped when he stepped closer. His bare skin felt hot, scorching against her back, the hard evidence of his arousal pressing against her buttocks.

He cupped her breasts as he pushed against her, his thumbs grazing over her nipples. Closing her eyes, she welcomed all the wonderful sensations. One hand drifted down to the apex of her thighs. As he nuzzled her neck, he whispered of all the things he wanted to do to her.

"Marcus," she murmured as she writhed against his fingers. "I can't wait. I need you. I need you now."

"Thank the Lord," he said, turning her to face him. He gulped as his gaze fell to her breasts. "Hell, I haven't the strength to hold back."

She marvelled at the sculptured muscles in his chest. She couldn't resist touching him, her fingers gliding over the hard planes, her gaze falling to stare at his jutting erection. "Good heavens."

Stepping forward, he snaked his arm around her back and pulled her close until she could feel the warmth radiating from his skin. "Now, where were we?"

He claimed her lips like a man possessed, devouring, delving deep inside, branding her with his hot mouth. Rampant hands seemed to cover every inch of her body.

"Forgive me," he gasped as he sucked in a breath. "I have a feeling this will be a frantic coupling as I don't have the patience to be thorough. At least, not this time."

"I don't care." She threaded her arms around his neck, pulled him closer, the thick shaft of pure masculine flesh pressing against her stomach. "I just want you. More than I have ever wanted anything."

He lowered her down onto the bed, covering her with his body. The time for talking had passed. The time for thinking about anything other than the pleasure rippling in waves, ready to carry her off to an exotic location had passed, too.

"I'll try to be gentle," he said, tormenting her with kisses on her neck, taking her nipple into his mouth and sucking.

"I'm fine. Just hurry, Marcus."

He needed no further inducement. Using his knee to coax her legs apart, he took himself in hand and pushed slowly inside her.

There were no words to describe the overwhelming sense of joy as she took him into her eager body.

"I'm not hurting you?"

"No … no. Not at all." She shook her head, wrapped her legs around him and relished in the glorious look of satisfaction etched on his face.

Withdrawing slowly, he filled her again and again, his thrusts growing harder, more determined. Following his pace, she rocked her hips to meet each moist slide.

"Oh, God, Anna." He focused his sinful gaze on her face. She stared into his warm brown eyes, showing him how much she welcomed his touch, showing him the ecstasy she felt building inside.

She arched her back, ran her hands over her breasts, threw her arms above her head with wanton abandon. He muttered something wicked as he held them there, held her captive, a slave to his rhythmical command. As the muscles in her stomach tightened, as the pulsing sensation brought her closer to some unknown destination, she thrashed and cried for more.

With a sudden spasm, her body shook, pulsing around the hard length of him. Every nerve tingled: she even felt it in her toes. Two more delicious strokes and he withdrew. A loud, masculine groan filled the room as took himself in hand.

The enchanting sound of their pants and ragged breathing warmed her soul.

Marcus collapsed on top of her. "You're mine." He growled the possessive words, and she knew then she had lost her heart to him.

CHAPTER 15

While Anna lay staring up at the ceiling, the gentleman at her side lay sprawled on his front sleeping soundly. Their second coupling, third if she counted the incident in the cave, had been just as wild, just as frantic. She resisted the urge to trace her finger along the three scars running across his back. Until a couple of days ago, the need to comfort any man had been foreign to her. Now she feared she would do anything to soothe his woes, secure his happiness.

You're mine!

His possessive words drifted through her mind, followed by a whole host of fanciful ideas—of her living in the monastery, of lying next to Marcus each night, of him loving her, protecting her.

Anna snorted and mentally shook her head.

What on earth had happened to her since leaving Labelles?

What had happened to the woman who wished for nothing more than to survive one more day? The one who wanted to live in solitude, hoping never to set eyes on another man again?

A noise in the corridor drew her gaze to the chamber door. With her mind being somewhat loud and chaotic, she wondered if she had imagined hearing the patter of footsteps. In her years at Labelles, she had been conditioned to listen out for distressing noises, which was why the soft whimpering captured her attention almost immediately.

Experience had taught her never to ignore a sorrowful sound.

Glancing at Marcus, she decided not to wake him; it was probably nothing. After spending numerous nights trailing the smugglers, he needed to sleep. There was also an element of self-preservation; she would not be able to resist him should he wake in an amorous mood, and she did not wish to appear too keen, too desperate for his attention.

Throwing on her chemise, she tied her cape around her shoulders and wrapped it across her chest. Only one candle lamp still flickered. The tiny wax stump would last for more than the few minutes needed to investigate the noise, she thought, as she picked it up and crept towards the door.

Why was it when one wanted to be quiet every sound seemed magnified? The click as she turned the iron key in the lock was louder than a hundred men cocking their pistols. The squeak as she eased the door gently from the jamb sounded like she had stumbled upon a hundred mice, all squealing at the sight of the unexpected giant figure.

Nonetheless, she managed to make it out into the corridor without disturbing Marcus.

The faint sobbing drifted through the air, but despite holding the lamp aloft, she could see nothing. The sound brought to mind the last time she had scoured the dimly lit hallways of Labelles, desperately trying to discover which one of her girls was crying. She had spent twenty minutes untying Amy's hands from the bedposts, rubbing her purple fingers until they were pink again.

Anna shook her head.

Had her guilt over the welfare of her girls played a part in her imagining the strange noises? She had no idea what had happened to them all. Whilst she had been busy enjoying the fair, chasing smugglers and lying enveloped in strong arms, heaven knows where they were or what fate lay in store for them. Anna hoped Lord Danesfield had kept his word. Indeed, she felt another measure of guilt for not telling him where he could find Miss Beaufort.

But she could never betray a trust.

Deciding she'd not be able to sleep until she had scanned the garth and chapel, Anna held her lamp high and wandered downstairs. Trying to listen for a noise amidst the stillness of the night was more difficult than one would imagine. A low humming resonated in her ears, convincing her she truly was a victim of her own wild imagination. But then she was not used to silence, particularly at night.

Memories.

Would she always be haunted by all the terrible things she'd heard and witnessed? Would she always—

Something caught her attention as she passed through the nave: a shadow hovering near the main door. An apparition shrouded in a long white cloak. Was this the source of the sorrowful sound? Feeling a frisson of fear, it crossed her mind to call out to Andre or Selene, but the words got lost in her throat.

Aware of her presence, the ghostly figure turned before racing out through the open door and into the night. Most women would have yelled or screamed, fled to their chamber to rouse masculine support. But Anna's inquisitive nature drew her to the door, forced her to peer out across the courtyard whilst her mind was busy trying to form an explanation for the bizarre events.

Had she seen a ghost?

Many old buildings claimed to have some form of resident spirit. One only had to read gothic novels to learn of mysterious hauntings though she doubted one would have the strength or the capability to lift the solid bar from the door.

What if Selene had ventured out? She knew of one girl who

had unlocked the front door and walked the length of three streets in her sleep.

Taking a few hesitant steps towards the stables, Anna heard the low neighs accompanied by the shuffling of hooves. Something had scared the horses. Perhaps she was wrong, and they had sensed an unusual force. Animals were known to be far more perceptive than people. However, in retrospect, she believed the mysterious figure must surely be a real person.

Had the smugglers seen them near the cave and followed them home? Was it their intention to frighten them to secure their silence?

No. Anna mentally shook her head. If they suspected someone knew of their criminal activities, surely their first thought would be to move the contraband. Without catching the smugglers in the act of transporting the goods, they had no proof. Besides, why would smugglers waste their time lurking in the stables?

In her mind that left only two options. Either, one of the servants was responsible or Victor's accomplice had discovered her whereabouts and had come looking for her.

Her heart thumped wildly in her chest.

She should run. She should race back into the monastery, bar the door and call Marcus. Indeed, she did turn and take a few steps towards the door. But stubbornness made her falter. By the time Marcus dressed and came down, the intruder would have scurried off into the night. She would be forever looking over her shoulder wondering when he would return. And she was tired of running and hiding. If someone lingered in the shadows, they could damn well show themselves.

With renewed determination she stormed into the stables. Lifting the lamp aloft once more, she scanned her surroundings. Nothing appeared unusual or out of place, and the horses seemed settled. Yet with a heightened sense of awareness and by the prickling feeling running down her spine, she knew she was not alone.

"You can come out now." Her tone conveyed an inner strength. It was not wise to show fear. Victor taught her that. "I saw you head in here."

The sound of someone tutting caused her to suppress a gasp. "Ah, Marie, night after night you keep me waiting. Why, when you knew I would come?"

Her heart shot up to her throat.

"Show yourself." Anna moved the lamp to the left and then the right but could see no one. The man must be hiding in one of the stalls, yet the horses were oddly calm.

"You enjoy playing your games with me." His thick French accent reminded her of the comte—a soft, friendly tone masking a stone-cold heart.

"Victor?" Even as the word left her lips, she knew it could not be true. She had seen him draw his last breath, had held the blood-stained knife in her hand. "Who … who are you? What do you want here?" Her frantic gaze scoured the shadows. "What do you want with me?"

"*Tout le monde sait que vous êtes une putain*. What do you think I want?"

In French, the vile words sounded venomous: *everyone knows you're a whore*. Fear struck at her heart. She had made a mistake leaving the safety of the monastery.

"Who are you?" she repeated shuffling back towards the door. As soon as he made a reply she would make a dash for it.

"What does it matter who—"

Anna did not wait to hear what he had to say.

As a man accustomed to sleeping lightly—when out in the field one could not take the risk of being set upon by brigands—Marcus heard Anna leave the room. Given the nature of her previous employment, one might make certain assumptions. Perhaps her girls were taught to make a distinction between bedding a man and sleeping with him. Had he been less confident in his ability to please or in the emotional connection they shared, he might have suspected an eagerness to return to her room.

Instinct told him something wasn't quite right.

Throwing on his breeches and shirt, he walked out into the corridor carrying his boots in his hand. Old habits had proved useful on numerous occasions; nothing hindered a man more than racing about barefooted in the dark.

"Miss Sinclair?" he whispered, rapping gently on her door. He did not bother to call out again and upon turning the handle and peering inside, realised the room stood empty.

Quickly expelling the slight hint of doubt that he may have mistaken the depth of her desire for him as a mere curiosity for frolicking, he thrust his feet into his boots and headed downstairs. Perhaps their rather exhaustive coupling had left her famished; he'd need to eat a whole pig to stop his grumbling stomach. The corners of his mouth curled up into a smile as his mind replayed various lascivious images.

God, he'd been desperate to bed her.

But the undeniably satisfying experience had left him craving her all the more. He had seriously underestimated the lure of an innocent. Indeed, he could not shake the feeling that she belonged with him now.

Bloody hell!

Tristan would roar with laughter if he were party to Marcus' thoughts.

Peering through the door into the refectory, he was certain Anna had not come in search of food. Then it occurred to him she might be in the chapel. A pang of guilt stabbed at his chest. Good Lord, he had taken her virginity. But how could he have possibly known the nature of her situation? Who had ever heard of a madam of a bawdy house being as pure as driven snow? It beggared belief.

As he passed through the nave, he spotted the open door.

Every muscle in his body went rigid. Why the hell would she venture outside in the middle of the night? Something definitely wasn't right.

Rushing over to investigate, he collided with the figure tearing through the door. Golden locks whipped his face as they both struggled to keep their balance.

"Anna?"

"Marcus?" Her eyes were wide, her gaze wild. One hand patted his chest roughly as though she feared he might be a figment of her imagination. "Quick, Marcus. Close the door. Quick. Hurry."

She placed the candle lamp on the floor and tugged at his arm.

"I'm closing it," he reassured, and as soon as the wooden bar was firmly in place she flew into his arms.

"I have never been more pleased to see you," she panted as she wrapped her arms around his waist. "Tell me you're real. Tell me I am not imagining it."

He lifted her chin and forced her to look at him. "What were you doing out there? What if Lenard's men had followed us home and were waiting for one of us to leave?" It was highly improbable but just saying the words caused panic to flare. "What if you'd tripped and hurt yourself and were lying on the cobblestones until morning?"

Marcus knew he sounded dramatic but the thought of her being out alone at night terrified him.

"I … I heard someone crying." She tried to calm her ragged breathing. "I heard footsteps outside your chamber. I saw someone in the nave, watched them race into the darkness."

Marcus frowned. “It was probably one of the servants. Why didn’t you wake me?”

She shook her head vigorously. “It wasn’t. Victor’s man has come for me.” She turned and stabbed her finger at the closed door. “He was out there, Marcus, waiting for me in the stables. I spoke to him.”

Marcus felt the blood drain from his face.

“Why the bloody hell didn’t you say so before?” Fear often manifested as anger. He threw the bar up as though it was as light as a twig.

Anna grabbed his arm. “Stay here. Don’t go out there.”

“If someone has been in this house, Anna, I want to know who it is. Stay here. Do not come out under any circumstances. If I fail to return within a few minutes, I want you to bar the door and fetch Andre.”

“Wait.”

Ignoring her plea, he tore across the courtyard, bursting into the stable. The horses snorted in response, their heads held high as they shuffled in their stalls. Marcus tried to keep calm. The last thing he needed was a kick from an irate stallion.

Hearing someone creeping behind him, he swung around violently, clenched his fist ready to knock the man to the floor.

“It’s me. It’s me,” Anna cried, holding her hands out in front of her as she shuffled back.

Marcus sighed and lowered his fist. “I told you to remain inside.”

“I couldn’t. I won’t let you get hurt because of me.”

Marcus didn’t know whether to be flattered or offended. “I’m more than capable of handling myself.”

“I know, I just …” She gave a little shrug as her luscious lips formed a pout.

“Come.” He took her hand, and they scoured the stables. “We’ll check all the outbuildings and then make a thorough search of the monastery.”

Once they were certain no one lurked in the shadows ready to pounce, they made their way inside.

"You said you spoke to him." Marcus bolted the door, replaced the heavy bar and turned to face her. "What did he say? Did he say he knew Victor?"

"No. But he called me Marie … he said … he said that everyone knows I am a whore."

Marcus gave a contemptuous snort as he brushed a tendril of hair from her face. "Then the man clearly doesn't know you at all."

She smiled at that, her blue eyes sparkling in the darkness, and he feigned a smile in return so as not to show his alarm. Other than Tristan, no one knew of her objectionable background. No one knew her as Marie. Indeed, she had insisted he introduce her as Anna Sinclair.

"Promise me you'll not leave the monastery without my knowledge," he continued, rubbing her upper arms as a way to soothe his tortured soul.

Promise me you'll never leave.

Shocked by the words penetrating his thoughts, he guided her away from the door.

"I promise," she murmured, stifling a yawn. "Now, where should we start?"

"Start?"

"Our search for the intruder."

He pondered her weary expression, stared at the dark shadows beneath her eyes. Only a fool would attempt to enter the building after being discovered. "Upstairs. We'll start with your room." Once secure, he would insist she lock the door behind her and get some sleep.

Thankfully, she did not question the flaws in his logic. But his conscience forced him to wake Andre and insist he rouse the other servants and make a thorough search of all the rooms downstairs.

As soon as they entered her room she rushed to the side table, picked up the brown leather Bible and gave a satisfied sigh as she hugged it to her chest.

"It holds some sentimental value, I assume?" He studied her as he tried to ignore the sweet smell of almonds that reminded him of the taste of her skin.

"It was a gift from my father." She offered him nothing more than that. Lifting the mattress, she ran her hand underneath and removed a white stocking. "And this is to help me start a new life."

Her comment hit him hard. The image of her settled somewhere else, with a husband oblivious to her past, annoyed him.

He walked over to her as she removed the roll of paper which he quickly realised was a large bundle of notes. "You should have told me you had money hidden up here. I have a vault downstairs. I could keep it safe for you."

She fingered the crisp paper. "I'll consider it. It's not that I don't trust you. I've always found it quite reassuring to keep it close."

They were the words of a person seeking any opportunity to escape. They were the words of a person longing for freedom. "Is that wise considering recent events?"

She sighed. "I doubt the intruder would attempt to enter the building again. But if anything should happen to me, Marcus, I would like you to give this to Lord Danesfield, to assist him in helping my girls."

He shook his head. "Nothing is going to happen to you, Anna. I will make sure of it." Marcus nodded to the money in her hand. "I assume you know how much is there?"

"Of course. Six hundred and forty pounds."

"Six hundred pounds!" It must have taken her years to save. The dissipated lords of London were obviously generous with their gifts to their host.

She shrugged. "It must last me a lifetime. If I'm frugal, I

should never need work again. If Victor had known of it, he would have killed me."

An icy chill ran down his spine.

She placed the notes on the bed and pulled another item out of her stocking. "I want you to sell this," she said, handing him a delicate brooch. "I have no notion of its value, but they're real diamonds not paste. I want you to spend the money on farming the land. I want you to consider finding another way to make your living."

To say he was astounded by her generosity was an understatement. "I will keep it safe for you, Anna. But as I've already stated, nothing is going to happen to you."

"You misunderstand me. I am giving you the brooch, Marcus, regardless of what the future may hold. I ask you to consider what I have said, but ultimately the choice is yours."

Marcus stared at the pretty object in his palm, the solid lump in his throat forcing him to suck in a breath. No one had ever given him anything. Indeed, all he had, he'd earned from trading or bartering information. He had come to learn that everything had a price; nothing was ever given freely.

Until today.

"I can't take it."

She covered his fingers with her own, curling them over the glittering jewel. "Yes. You can. I want you to have it. The purpose of an heirloom is to enhance the life of the recipient, to serve as a memory of the person who left it behind. In giving me sanctuary here, you have enhanced my life, and I always repay my debts." She chuckled sweetly, the sound an obvious attempt to placate him.

He didn't need money. But it would be rude and ungrateful to refuse after such a heartfelt plea, and he sensed it was important to her. He would find a way to compensate her for the thoughtful gesture.

But how could he accept her precious gift knowing what he was about to do?

To keep her safe, he needed to know everything about the business dealings of the Comte de Dampierre. Was there an accomplice? When it came to business and delving into people's affairs, Dudley Spencer was more adept at uncovering information.

Dudley's price would be high, of course.

The price would be information regarding Miss Beaufort's secret hideaway. The price would be a little cottage in the village of Marlow, somewhere near a church, he suspected.

CHAPTER 16

"Take this to your father come first light," Marcus said, handing the letter to a tired-looking Selene. "Tell him to send it as a matter of urgency." He sat back in the chair behind his desk and surveyed the five solemn faces.

"We have searched every room, Mr. Danbury." Andre shook his head and shrugged. "There is no one here. I am sure of it."

It was as he suspected.

Someone had found a way into his home, and it did not sit well with Marcus. "You searched every room, the warming room, the pot house?"

Andre nodded and then jerked his head to the man on his left. "Justin checked them all twice, made sure the windows were secure, checked for any sign of entry."

Justin plastered his hand over his mouth to stifle a yawn. "I did, Mr. Danbury."

"And what of Selene's and Matilda's room?"

"Andre, he even searched behind the armoire," Selene murmured.

"Very well." Marcus sighed. Once they had all returned to their beds, he would check again for any sign of forced entry.

Just to be certain. He turned his attention to Selene. "I suggest you take Justin with you when you go down to the village. It would not be wise for a woman to walk alone until we know who we're dealing with."

Selene lowered her gaze. "Forgive me. But perhaps … perhaps Miss Sinclair was mistaken. Dreams can sometimes seem so real … *si vives* … so vivid."

Had they been talking about any other woman, Marcus might have considered the possibility. But Anna was no simpering miss. She had witnessed the worst kind of depravity, experienced the most terrifying abuse. Her courage knew no bounds. Unlike most women of his acquaintance, she did not have to lie or invent silly stories to get attention.

Marcus straightened. "If Miss Sinclair says she saw someone running out of the monastery, if she says she spoke to a man in the stables, then I believe her."

Selene nodded as she glanced at the floor. "*Oui*. Of course."

"Now." Marcus stood and brushed his hand through his hair. "It's just a few hours until dawn. You had all better get yourselves back to bed. But stay alert. I want to know the moment you encounter anything suspicious, hear a noise, discover something out of place, anything."

His staff nodded, and collectively muttered 'Yes, Mr. Danbury' as they vacated the room.

Marcus remained standing, his mind preoccupied with the night's events. Was Anna really in any danger? Or had the intruder used intimate knowledge of her situation to divert their suspicions away from his real objective.

Bloody hell.

After putting an end to many nefarious plots over the years, numerous men could have broken into his home as a means to exact their revenge. He had always known the day would come. Until now, he hadn't given the matter much thought. When one possessed a certain skill in the art of pugilism, was adept with a sword and an accurate shot with a pistol, there was no need for concern.

So why did he feel like tracking down every suspect and stringing them up from the nearest tree?

Anna.

With no family, no responsibilities, he had never given a damn for his own safety. He had accepted his fate a long time ago. With his type of work, one never presumed they'd live to see the sun rise. Perversely, he almost wished the day would come. Should anything happen to him, he knew his father would blame himself for Marcus' death. When the time came for him to draw his last breath, the knowledge would bring him comfort. Anything that caused his father to suffer was worth the pain.

But now things had changed.

Now he felt responsible for another.

Not in the way he felt about Tristan—he would give his life for the man who'd been his loyal friend and constant companion. He would give his life for Anna, too, he suddenly realised. But as each day passed, the thought of living in the monastery without her, the thought of not having her in his life—

Damn it all. Dane had a lot to answer for. Indeed, he made a mental note to punch him hard on the nose the next time he laid eyes on him.

Pushing away from his desk, he picked up the candle and strode out under the shelter of the cloisters. With dawn fast approaching, there was little point sleeping, and so he retraced Anna's steps, searched for anything untoward.

Just as Andre had said, Marcus found no sign of forced entry. Despite various reports to the contrary, he had never found any sign of a secret entrance either.

Now, he would have to pursue another line of enquiry—one that left an empty, hollow feeling in his gut.

A member of his staff had let the intruder into his home.

It was the only feasible explanation. But why?

With a heavy sigh, he trudged upstairs, hovered outside Anna's door not knowing quite what to do. He would not reveal his suspicion: primarily because he did not want to alert the culprit. And he did not want Anna to worry. She had spent years looking over her shoulder, not knowing whom she could trust. He would not have her living in fear, not in his house.

No, he could not abide disloyalty and would secretly investigate the matter until he found the person responsible.

As though sensing his presence, she opened the door ajar and peered around. "I heard footsteps. Is everything all right?"

Damn. He did not want her to think he was insensitive, that he lingered with lascivious intentions in mind. "I have finished searching the house but couldn't sleep. Forgive me, if my prowling disturbed you."

She smiled, opened the door a little wider, and he was somewhat disappointed to see her soft curves shrouded in a cotton nightgown. "I couldn't sleep, either. I keep thinking about what he said to me. How he knew my name."

They stared into each other's eyes for a moment; his deep sense of longing reflected back at him, and he suspected their thoughts followed a similar vein.

"If you want company, you only have to say." Being the first to find the courage to speak, he added, "We could sit in the chapter house and read. You can tell me why you think I should farm the land."

Her eyes brightened. "Or you … you could come in. We could lie together, try to get a few hours' sleep."

Desire ignited, but he imagined dousing the flames with ice-cold water. She did not need him to fawn over her. She needed comfort, kindness, and a few hours of peace. "Very well," he nodded, and she stepped back for him to enter.

~

Later that night they rode down to the village.

"By the sound of it, a large number of people have decided to venture out this evening." Anna glanced across the road at the bustling inn, noting the sound of jovial singing and the golden glow spilling out of every window. "Tell me again what we're doing here?"

Marcus pulled her back into the shadows. Even in the dim light, his eyes sparkled with mischief, with a wicked sensuality. "We're here to enjoy ourselves, relax and have a drink."

"This time, I do not need to pretend to be your mistress." She felt her face flame as the words left her lips. The memory of their coupling warmed her heart. The memory of the hours spent sleeping in each other's arms warmed her soul.

"Don't say it like that." His tone held a hint of reproof. "You're not my mistress, Anna. The word implies something undignified, something shallow and self-serving, and in no way defines what we've shared."

Her heart fluttered at his response. Was he trying to be kind or had their joining meant something to him, too? Could he ever care for her the way she cared for him?

"I simply meant things are different now." She refused to say anything more. To explore the topic of conversation might lead her to divulge her true feelings and she couldn't think about that now. "Besides, I thought we were here to investigate. I thought you were desperate to discover the identity of the intruder."

"We're here to relax and observe. To wait for the culprit to reveal himself."

"I doubt he's going to jump up, throw his hands in the air and confess all," she said as they stared at the stone building. While she saw the logic in Marcus' plan, the likelihood of finding the comte's accomplice sitting in full view of half the village was minimal at best.

"Obviously not, but I've often found the criminal mind to be rather predictable. Where best to find information than an inn full of loose-mouthed drunkards?"

Anna gasped. "You think Victor's accomplice has been staying here, that he has talked to the villagers?" How she managed to get the words out without shrieking was a mystery. The blackguard could have been watching her for days. The thought caused her to shiver, and Marcus drew the edges of her cape tightly across her chest, rubbed her upper arms.

"We don't know if the intruder is Victor's accomplice." He raised his hand when she opened her mouth to protest. "I know what you're going to say, that he must be, else how could he have known your name, your previous occupation."

"Exactly," she said with an element of frustration. "There is no other explanation."

A frisson of fear shot through her as she realised the gravity of her words. A man, just as cold and as callous as Victor, had come to seek his revenge.

Marcus raised an arrogant brow. "There is always another explanation, and more often than not it is glaringly obvious. We've missed a vital piece of the puzzle and tonight a casual conversation will lead us to the culprit."

"You seem mighty confident. I just hope you're right."

"I'm always right," he said with a chuckle. "Besides, if you think about it logically, the accomplice would have had to have been in London on the night Victor died. He would have had to have followed you here."

Anna tried to recall the events of the night she stabbed Victor. For her own sanity, she had hoped never to revisit them. Lord Danesfield had been busy arranging her departure. He had ridden alongside the carriage, stayed with them until they'd set sail. Fragments of memories flashed through her mind. Had they been followed? She didn't think so. Then again, her thoughts had been in a state of constant disarray.

"I don't remember seeing anyone lurking about, but I'm certain Lord Danesfield would have noticed."

Marcus nodded. "Precisely. Dane would have known the moment someone started trailing your carriage. And if the accomplice did follow you here why wait three weeks to reveal himself? You've been down to the village numerous times on your own. He's had every opportunity to approach you before now."

Anna pondered his words. "I suppose it does sound a little far-fetched. But there is another option. What if he came looking for Victor at Labelles, heard of Lord Danesfield's involvement from one of the girls and found a way to read his letters?"

Marcus massaged his chin, the furrow between his brows growing more prominent. "It's nigh on impossible. The letters were all stamped with Dane's crest." He paused. "Unless he stole one, intercepted it *en route* somehow."

She had not thought of that. "So you believe there is a possibility the man in the stable could be Victor's accomplice?"

He stroked her cheek, the affectionate gesture calming her racing heart. "Look. We must not jump to conclusions. We must study the facts as they present themselves. I've written to Dudley Spencer, Dane's associate, and asked him to investigate the matter of the comte having a business partner. But it could take weeks for him to write back with news. In the meantime, we must see what we can discover for ourselves."

Anna forced a smile. Regardless of her earlier reservations, she trusted his decision. Besides, she enjoyed his company and the thought of spending a few leisurely hours with him was reward in itself.

They crossed the road to the inn. Marcus opened the door for her, and they walked inside. As she suspected, the place was full to bursting, every table occupied, the boisterous throng all singing along with a minstrel strumming his lute. Various smells flooded her senses: wood smoke mingled with stale tobacco, sweat and beef stew. It took a tremendous amount of effort not to cover her nose and gag.

Nodding to the few people who offered a greeting, she scanned the room. "Did you know it would be this busy?"

"One of the minstrels stayed on after the fair. I heard he has developed an affection for Lenard's sister."

Anna cast him a sidelong glance. Was that the reason for their visit? Was Marcus distrusting of the stranger amongst their midst?

"Well, he's certainly brought some life to the place," she said, deciding not to broach the subject of the intruder again.

Just being in Marcus' company made her anxieties disappear. She tried to imagine what his life would be like without the thrill of an assignment—safer, predictable, rather dull? As much as she'd been keen for him to abandon his dangerous pursuits and farm the land, she felt he would need a purpose, a cause worth fighting for if he was to be truly happy.

An idea popped into her head, one as illuminating as a hundred candles in a dark room. Wonderful! She knew just the thing. Indeed, if Marcus showed no interest in the project, she would fund it herself. All she needed—

"Madame Tullier is beckoning us to her table," Marcus said, tapping her on the arm to disturb her reverie.

She followed Marcus' gaze to the middle-aged woman sitting to their right in the near corner of the room. Anna watched her take an empty chair from the table next to her before looking up and waving vigorously enough to fan a spark into a flame.

Pushing past the people standing, they made their way to the woman whose pastries were so delicious they would sell for a shilling a piece in London. Born and raised in Whitechapel before marrying a Frenchman at the tender age of sixteen, Madame Tullier had lived in the village for thirty years.

"Sit 'ere," she said with some excitement. The woman liked

talking about England, but usually, it took a few sentences before she reverted to her natural dialect.

"I shall go and get a drink," Marcus said, pulling out a chair for Anna to sit.

Anna looked up at his handsome face. "I think that would be wise considering the number of people in here tonight."

"I'm so pleased for Lenard," Madame Tullier said when Marcus left them alone. "Fate has a way of bringin' an answer to all our prayers."

Anna nodded as she offered the woman a warm smile, suddenly realising that the same was true of her situation. "I couldn't agree with you more, *madame*."

Fate had brought her to Marcus Danbury, to the delightful monastery where she had discovered the true nature of the person hidden within—the person she had buried beneath a false facade for far too long.

"Lucy, you must call me Lucy." She nodded to a point beyond Anna's shoulder. "Antoine had the same idea about the drinks though it's been a while since he's looked at me the way Mr. Danbury does you. You can always tell the look of a gentleman in love, I say."

Anna swallowed deeply. All the blood rushed to her cheeks, and she pressed them with the tips of her fingers. The woman had obviously mistaken a friendly countenance for something far more meaningful.

"My, it's hot in here," Lucy said, giving her a knowing wink as she removed her shawl. "It's so hot it's made my heart all aflutter."

"Mr. Danbury mentioned the minstrel had brought people out this evening," Anna said in a desperate attempt to change the subject. Removing her cape and draping it over her chair, she asked, "What made the minstrel decide to stay? Mr. Danbury thought it had something to do with Lenard's sister."

Lucy nodded. "Juliet? She was widowed last spring. But for

a woman with her warmth an' natural beauty, I'm not surprised she's found love again. That's why I'm so pleased for Lenard. He's such a good man and deserves some happy news."

Anna pitied the woman's naiveté. If only she knew the man she spoke highly of was planning to ship contraband across the sea.

"Well, I'll be surprised if he doesn't run out of ale tonight," Anna said in a neutral tone.

Lucy Tullier shrugged. "I'm sure he won't mind. No ale means a pocket full of coin and he needs it more than anyone. Bless his soul."

Intrigued by the comment, Anna glanced over her shoulder before turning back to her companion. "I would imagine he makes a decent enough living here. I didn't realise he was struggling financially."

Lucy Tullier leant across the table, the wooden surface supporting her large bosom. "Don't say it was me as told you, but his daughter has got this problem with her bones. The doctor said he's got to break her leg and reset it else she'll not walk properly again."

"But I didn't even know he had a daughter. I mean, I've never seen her about the village."

"She stays in her room, mostly. Lenard confided in Antoine but don't mention—" Lucy Tullier stopped abruptly as Marcus and Antoine returned with mugs of ale.

Lost in thoughtful contemplation, Anna jumped when Marcus tapped her on the arm.

"They've no wine, so I bought you ale," he said, sitting in the chair beside her. "I can take it back."

"It doesn't matter. I'm sure it will be fine." She shook her head, offering a smile to reassure him. Besides, her mind was too preoccupied with a moral dilemma to worry about her own needs. Lenard's involvement with the smugglers was a means to fund his daughter's care.

"It's good to see everyone enjoying themselves," Marcus said, after taking a sip of his ale. "I know almost everyone here, except the man propped up against the wooden pillar." Marcus jerked his head. "The one with the wavy black hair and long side-whiskers."

Both Lucy and Antoine glanced covertly at the stranger. Anna stared, too, doubting the scrawny excuse for a man could be Victor's accomplice.

"Do you mean Samuel? The man smoking the clay pipe?"

Marcus nodded.

"Ah, but you must know Samuel," Antoine said with some surprise. "He has been working in Lyon these past few years, something to do with Italy and the silk trade. I have seen him about a few times this week and assumed he'd come home to stay."

Marcus shook his head. "I have a reasonably good memory, but I can't recall ever meeting him before."

Antoine threw his hands up in the air. "Ah, you must have. Samuel Lessard. His sister Selene is your cook."

CHAPTER 17

"Is everything all right?" Anna said as they entered the chapter house. She removed her cape and draped it over the chair. "You hardly said a word on the ride home. Indeed, you've been quiet ever since Antoine mentioned Selene's brother."

Marcus could think of nothing other than Samuel Lessard. The man had left the inn shortly after their arrival. His return to the village and the fact his sister worked at the monastery could not be a coincidence. Marcus suspected one of his staff had caused the disturbance which caused Anna to leave his room to investigate. Despite his suspicion, he could not imagine Selene would have either the courage or the cunning required to achieve the task.

"I'm curious to know more about any newcomers to the village. But I was thinking about what happened here last night. I've been replaying the event over in my mind." He lit the candelabra and gestured for her to sit. "Tell me again what you heard, what you saw. Leave nothing out. Tell me everything, even the insignificant details."

He sat back in the chair behind his desk. The distance would allow him to focus on the task. Being alone with Anna always caused desire to flare, and he was forced to banish all thoughts of seduction.

She sat in the chair opposite. “I heard footsteps pacing the corridor outside your room.”

She had only just begun, and a question popped into his head. “When you say footsteps, be more precise. Were they heavy like the dull thud of boots, or light like the patter of bare feet?”

She pursed her lips, the lines on her brow more prominent as she glanced up at the ceiling. “They were light, so light I almost missed them.”

Marcus nodded. The revelation did not bode well for Selene. “And you didn’t think to wake me?”

“You were tired.” She shrugged, and a tempting smile played at the corners of her mouth. “You were sleeping so soundly, and I am used to leaving my room in the middle of the night to check on the girls, to console and offer words of comfort.”

Marcus swallowed down the hard lump in his throat as he imagined her dealing with all sorts of distressing scenarios. “You said you heard whimpering. Was it the sound of someone in pain, or a more mournful cry?”

She glanced at the floor in silent contemplation. “I’m not sure. I remember thinking it sounded sorrowful, but when I saw the apparition, then it became a grieving wail.”

Marcus straightened. “Apparition? But you said you didn’t see the man who spoke to you.” He could have kicked himself for not pursuing the matter earlier. But he had been so angry with her, so damn scared of some mysterious accomplice seeking revenge.

“It was more a white shrouded figure,” she said calmly, yet he wanted to shake her, demand to know why she’d not mentioned it before. “I only saw it briefly. For a second, I thought it was a ghost. Indeed, when I followed it through the main door out into the night, it disappeared."

Marcus stroked his chin as he contemplated her words. "When you say a white figure, I assume the person wore light-coloured clothing?"

"Again, I can't be sure. It was similar to a cape, something long, floaty and white. And it had a hood."

Marcus sat forward. "What did your instincts tell you? Did you believe you had seen a ghost?"

Anna shook her head. "My first thought was that it could have been Andre or Selene. I have known of people walking in their sleep for miles without waking and well …"

It was as he suspected. One of his staff had lured her outside. Marcus would question them all again come first light.

"You're certain the man you spoke to was French, that he used your name?"

"Definitely. He sounded so like … like Victor." Her face turned ashen, and her bottom lip quivered. "I … I once told Miss Beaufort that Victor would find me no matter where I went. That there wasn't a place in the world where I would be safe. I … I thought he'd found me, Marcus. I thought he'd come to drag me back to the nightmare, which sounds ridiculous when you consider the fact he's dead. But what if it's true? What if he has come back to haunt me?"

She sucked in a breath. His heart lurched as a solitary tear trickled down her cheek. Before he knew what he was doing, he moved around the desk and pulled her to her feet to hold her tightly in his arms.

"I promise you'll never have to fear him again. I'm here for you." He almost choked on the sudden wave of emotion surging up to his throat. "I shall be your protector, the person who wipes away your tears. The person who makes you smile. The person who makes you forget all about the horrors of the past."

When she looked up at him, her eyes were brimming with

hope, yet still tinged with sorrow. "I have prayed for you for so long. I have prayed to the Lord, for him to show me the way. Now when I am with you, I feel whole again."

Her words touched him. He felt a better person in her company. Until now, it had not occurred to him that he had used his assignments as a way to fill the emptiness, as a way to banish the loneliness.

"I have been waiting for you, too," he managed to say as the need to bury himself deep inside her luscious body took hold.

She shook her head and gave a weak chuckle. "Never in my wildest dreams did I ever believe I would find someone I could trust. Someone I could depend upon."

Guilt drove a spear right through his deceitful heart.

At some point, he would have to tell her what he'd done. He would tell her that he had betrayed her trust, divulged information she had unwittingly shared. But now only one thing could force the Devil from his door.

"I need you." They were words he had never spoken to another. Words that he never imagined would fall so easily from his lips.

She replied with her body, pressing into him until he could feel the shape of her soft breasts squashed against his chest. She replied with her mouth, standing on the tips of her toes to claim his.

There was nothing sweet, nothing tame about the way they revealed their need for each other. With loud pants and guttural groans, he devoured her, plunged deep inside her mouth, their shared breath like a potent elixir. He tasted her over and over until every memory before her dissolved into nothing.

She was his life now.

He recognised the truth of it.

Without breaking contact, they shuffled to the door. He tore his lips away to turn the key in the lock. Frantic hands stripped him of his waistcoat, of his shirt, ran over his bare chest as though it was something wondrous to behold.

Drunk with desire, he did not think of their comfort, or for the need to preserve their clothing. Buttons hit the floor. He heard the sound of stitching ripped apart from seams. There was no time to prepare her, to sweeten the moment, to make it easier to claim her body.

God, he'd never been so desperate to bury himself inside a woman. He had never been so hard in his entire life.

Naked and locked in a passionate embrace, they writhed on the floor, possessed by an urgency to be joined, to cement the powerful feelings that would bind them forever. When he entered her with one long thrust, they both cried out—with relief, with pleasure, with the agonising truth that this still would not be enough for either of them.

"Please, Marcus," she panted as she wrapped her legs around him, dug her nails into his buttocks. "Make me forget."

A fierce hunger drove him on, pushing him harder. The thought of ensuring her pleasure fluttered through his mind and without a word, he slipped his arm beneath her and flipped them over.

"What … what are you doing?"

He cursed for not thinking of it sooner. Above him, with her honey-gold hair hanging loosely around her shoulders and her small round breasts that were a perfect fit for his palms, she looked like a goddess sent to lure mortal men into a life of debauchery and sin.

"Move with me," he instructed, his hands settling on the soft curve of her hips. "Like this." He groaned as the muscles in her core hugged him tight.

Her face flushed. But as soon as he moved inside her, she abandoned all reservations and with his help settled into a steady rhythm.

His fingers found her sweet spot, and he stroked back and

forth, fighting desperately against the need to thrust hard. He loved the way she moved with him, loved the glazed look in her eyes that overshadowed the pain and sorrow.

Her movements grew more desperate as the passion he could feel deep within drove her forward. Her breath came fast. The short pants breezing out of her parted lips were like music for the soul.

"*Marcus.*"

As soon as the first shudder shook her, he flipped her back over again and drove hard and quick.

"*Bloody hell.*" The whispered words were accompanied by his roar of satisfaction as he withdrew just in time to spill his seed over her stomach.

They lay on the floor, her head on his chest, his arm draped around her shoulder as his fingers traced light circles on her back. It had been the hurried coupling of a man in his youth. But it had brought a level of satisfaction to surpass all else. And as his breathing settled and the soft pulse of sated desire ebbed, he tried to address his feelings.

He was in love with her.

It wasn't a shocking revelation. He had known from the very beginning, from the moment Tristan helped her down from the carriage and their eyes had met. Perhaps even before then, even before he knew of her existence. Somehow he had always known they would meet, and his life would take a new direction. He would have a new, infinitely more rewarding purpose.

And that was why he could not deceive her.

If they had any hope of creating a future together, then it must be built on honesty, trust, and respect.

"There is something I need to tell you," he heard himself say before the logical part of his brain protested. The shiver that rippled through her body shook him, too.

"Judging by your rather grave tone, I suspect that whatever it is it won't be pleasant." Trembling fingers on his chest belied her playful tone. "Just give me a moment to dress."

As he threw on his shirt and breeches, he could sense her pulling away from him, emotionally withdrawing as a means of protection. Each layer of clothing covering her body acted as a barrier to reinforce her defences. An uncomfortable silence filled the room, the air around them feeling heavier, denser.

"Does it have something to do with the minstrel, with Samuel Lessard or Lenard?" she asked apprehensively. "Lucy Tullier told me about Lenard's problems with his daughter, and I can't help thinking that's why he's involved in smuggling."

Marcus frowned. After the recent turn of events, he had almost forgotten about the smugglers. "I know his daughter keeps to her room, but he never mentioned why."

Anna attempted to brush the creases from the front of her dress. "His daughter is ill. The doctor wants to break her leg and reset it. I assume the bill is more than Lenard can afford."

"Why do I get the sense you're chastising me for a misdemeanour?" He threw his hands in the air. "What do you want me to do, Anna? Ignore the crime? Tell Coombes I was mistaken when I informed him they were ready to ship out?"

She stepped closer. "Should you not take his circumstances into account, Marcus? The man must be beside himself with worry. Could you not speak to him and explain the danger he faces?"

"And let the whole village know I'm an impostor?"

"You could make them understand," she implored.

Damn it all. How had they progressed from the most satisfying moment of his entire life to the most frustrating conversation he had ever been party to?

"Look. This is not about Lenard or Lessard or the blasted minstrel." Anger infused his tone. But it stemmed from a gut-wrenching fear of revealing the real depth of his betrayal.

"Well, what is it about then?" she said haughtily.

Marcus sighed, although the long drawn out sound did nothing to ease his anxiety.

He had no idea how to broach the subject, but he knew he needed to make her understand the bond he shared with Dane. "Whenever I've taken on a new assignment, I've always known there's a chance I could lose my life. When you work so closely with other gentlemen you develop a code of honour. You learn to depend on them. Indeed, Dane bears a scar on his chest. A scar he received whilst defending me."

Anna shook her head. "If you're telling me Lord Danesfield saved your life, then after what I've witnessed I am not surprised." She gave an indifferent shrug. "But I don't understand why you're telling me?"

"I owe Dane and his associate, Dudley Spencer, a debt. They assisted me when it mattered most, and I am duty bound to do the same." He brushed his hands through his hair as he paced the floor to stop his racing heart from shooting up to his throat. "I just want you to understand the implications of such a debt."

"Why do I get the sense you're preparing me for something? What is it you wish to tell me?" she asked, and he did not need to look at her to know her eyes were wide or to know fear had replaced the look of wonder he'd seen just a few moments earlier.

"Dudley wrote to me. He wants to know where he can find Miss Beaufort." He almost gasped with relief when he'd finally spoken the words. "You must know, my only thought was to protect you. When you told me you'd spoken to Victor's accomplice, I feared the worst."

When he found the courage to look into her enchanting blue eyes, he could see pain; he could see sorrow.

"What have you done, Marcus?" He heard a trace of disdain in her voice.

He took a deep breath. "I told Dudley I would exchange information. I would reveal what I know of Miss Beaufort's whereabouts. In return, he will discover all he can of Victor's accomplice."

She shook her head and laughed. "But it is of no consequence as you do not know where Miss Beaufort is. And I would never break a trust in a bid to save myself. Surely, after what has passed between us, you must know that of me."

"God damn it, Anna. I know where Miss Beaufort is." Shame and guilt fuelled his anger now. "One does not have to be skilled in the art of manipulation. It is a simple case of piecing together the facts."

Her mouth fell open, and she stepped away from him, her hand coming up to cover her heart. "But I haven't said a thing about Miss Beaufort. You couldn't possibly know—"

"I told Dudley to search the village of Marlow near High Wycombe. I told him to look for a cottage next to the church."

Marcus had experienced pain many times in his life: physical pain in the form of severe beatings. Indeed, he still bore the scars on his back. Emotional pain in the form of losing the only person who had ever mattered to him. But he had never experienced anything like the torturous feeling when witnessing the look of disappointment on Anna's face.

"You … you told him about Marlow, even though you knew my feelings on the matter?" She shuffled back, gulped, gasped for breath. "You betrayed my trust. You let me believe in you. You let me believe in us." She waved her hand back and forth between them, but the corners of her mouth curled down in contempt.

"I did it for you." His argument sounded weak, a pathetic attempt to justify his actions.

"You should have given me the opportunity to decide what was best." A tear trickled down her cheek. "Do you know what Miss Beaufort went through because of me? I came to the aid of a girl, a girl who reminded me of myself in every way. As a consequence, Miss Beaufort almost lost her life, almost became the property of a depraved madman. Do you have any idea what would have happened to her if Victor had got his way?"

"But Dane is in love with her. He has no intention of hurting her, just as I have no intention of hurting you."

Anna snorted, waved her hand to the floor, to the place where they had consummated their love. "Lying with a man is not love. Trusting a man, knowing he has your interests at heart, that you can always depend on him, that is love. Miss Beaufort wanted time to think, time to consider what she truly wants. Not what society dictates. Not what serves Victor, Lord Danesfield or her brother!"

"I was thinking of you," he repeated as he closed his eyes briefly.

"No, Marcus. You were thinking of your duty to your comrades. You ignored my wishes. You deceived me into believing I could trust you, into believing there was hope for … for …"

A sob broke suddenly, and she could not finish the sentence. Without another word, she turned and fled.

"Anna!"

Marcus did not go after her. She needed time to accept that her welfare had been the only motivating factor in his decision. She needed time to realise he was not Victor, not an evil monster of a man, but a man in love.

A man who would sell his soul to save her.

A man who would turn his back on everything he'd ever known for a chance to put it right.

CHAPTER 18

Anna ran through the cloisters, tears streaming down her face. They were the unshed tears of the innocent girl from Marlow. They were tears for all the unbearable days and nights she had spent at the mercy of a cold-hearted devil. They were the painful tears of heartbreak, of knowing the wonderful dream one always hoped for would never come to pass.

She knew of only one place she could go.

A chill breezed over her as she entered the chapel. Despite the darkness, there was an illuminating presence in the small room. She stared at the stained glass window, at the figure looking up to the heavens, at the golden glow surrounding him, and tried to rouse just a flicker of faith.

But she felt nothing.

How could she when the Lord refused to grant her even the smallest mercy? Perhaps she only had herself to blame. Sinners were supposed to repent. An image of Marcus nestled between her thighs flashed into her mind. In the eyes of some, she truly was a whore. But she had given herself to a man she loved.

Was that so wrong?

"Give me a sign," she whispered as she put her hands

together in prayer and tried to regulate her breathing. "Show me the way. Tell me what to do."

She did not expect to see a host of angels; she did not expect to hear the rapturous sound of a harp or to feel her soul soar. But she heard her name echoing in her mind.

Marie Labelle ... Anna Sinclair.

She stopped being Marie Labelle the moment she thrust the knife into Victor's back. In truth, she stopped being Anna Sinclair the moment she accepted the position of governess to a lying scoundrel.

She despised both of them for being so weak, so vulnerable, for bowing so easily to the demands and desires of men. As if it wasn't enough to have two women competing for prominence, now she had a third.

Now she had the woman who had come to an old monastery, who had fallen in love, allowed her lover to see the real person hidden inside. The woman who had lost more than her freedom or reputation. The woman who had lost her heart.

Then the answer came to her.

She had to leave. She had to go as far away as she could. She could not reclaim her reputation or her heart, but she could reclaim her freedom.

Without allowing any other thought to penetrate her addled mind, she raced to her room. There was no time to pack the few meagre belongings. All she needed was her Bible, money and her thick cape.

But her most prized possession was not on the side table. Frantically, she searched the floor, under pillows, in drawers. Panic flared.

Her mind replayed the moment she had last held it in her hand.

Shaking her head, she rushed along the corridor to the room at the end of the hall. Barging into Marcus' private quarters without knocking, she scoured the chamber. Where else could it be? Who else would know of her attachment to it?

Anna heard the thud of booted footsteps coming towards her. Marcus appeared in the doorway. Her heart lurched. She wanted to run into his arms and forget all about the cottage in Marlow, pretend she'd never heard his confession.

But she was tired of being weak and merciful.

"Where is it?" she blurted before he could ask what she was doing rummaging around in his drawers. "What have you done with it?"

Marcus shrugged. "With what?"

"My Bible. Don't pretend you don't know what I mean. The brown leather-bound book I keep by my bed."

Her pulse was racing; her throat felt tight. Each word sounded more croaky than the last.

Marcus frowned as he stepped into the room. "Why would I have it? Why would you think it is in here? What motive would I have for taking it?"

Distrust flowed like hot lava through her veins, consuming what remained of all logical thought. She raised her chin. "Perhaps you were the one I heard that night in the stables? You're the only one who knows my name. You're the only one who knows of my previous profession. Perhaps you thought by scaring me I'd be forced to trust you. And then I would tell you what you want to know. I would tell you where to find Miss Beaufort so you could run back to your friend and act the dutiful hero."

The muscles in his jaw twitched as his expression darkened. He raised an arrogant brow. "If you believe me capable of such a heinous crime, then why are you still here? I'm not forcing you to stay. I can write to Dane and ask him to make alternative arrangements."

His cold tone hurt her like a sharp slap to the face. The shock made her reconsider her harsh words. But she could not retract them; she could not bow and scrape to him.

"I don't need a man to make arrangements for me. I am more than capable of taking care of myself."

With his mouth set in a firm line, he stepped back. Pride forced her to walk past him. In the morning, she would go down to the village, see Lucy Tullier or ask Lenard if there were any rooms at the inn. The man obviously needed the money. Perhaps she could set sail with the smugglers and ask them to leave her in Guernsey.

Feeling a little nauseous and with her mind replaying the events of the evening, she struggled to sleep. She heard Marcus pacing back and forth along the length of the corridor, his heavy gait evidence of his sour mood. A few times, he stopped outside her door, the silence almost deafening while she waited to see if he would knock.

She supposed she had been quite scathing in her outburst. Of course, she knew he was not the man she'd heard in the stables. But Marcus had betrayed her. How could she ever trust him again? No doubt, he would use her bitter accusation against her to ease the burden of his own guilt.

The bright morning sun streaming in through her window did nothing to relieve her chaotic mind and aching body. Nausea had progressed into a stabbing pain just behind her navel, and she felt hot, short of breath. Perhaps it had something to do with the ale she'd drunk at the inn. Perhaps this was the pain of heartbreak.

After hiding in her room all morning, Anna plucked up the courage to go and speak to Marcus, and so made her way downstairs. Whatever happened between them, she was grateful for his hospitality and could not leave without explaining her plans. The thought caused her stomach to lurch. Hopefully, Selene would know of something to ease the pain. She was a marvel when it came to plants and herbs. The balm she'd made for

Anna's hands had worked a treat. They were almost as soft and smooth as when she'd first arrived.

Anna spotted the woman coming out of the chapter house. "Selene."

"*Oui, madame*?"

"Do you happen to know of something I can take to settle my stomach?" The mere thought of a remedy caused another sharp pang, and she rubbed the area with her palm. "I don't think ale agrees with me."

Selene frowned. "Is there a headache, a sickness or fever?" She put her hand out to touch Anna's forehead but left it hanging in the air until Anna nodded to give her consent. "You feel hot. I shall go and fetch a tonic."

Anna gave a sigh of relief. "Is Mr. Danbury feeling well?" she said, gesturing to the closed door. They had shared the same meal, drunk the same ale.

"Oh, he is not here. He asked me to tidy the room."

"Did he say where he was going?" Anna wondered if his absence had anything to do with their argument last night.

"*Non*, *madame*. He left over an hour ago."

Anna sighed as she touched her fingers to her temple, the pressure going some way to relieve the pounding. "I'll take a tonic, and then I think I'll go for a walk. Do you need anything from the village? I have a few errands to run." Finding somewhere else to stay was her priority.

Selene shook her head. "Mr. Danbury says you are not to go out on your own. And you are not well, I fear."

When she spoke to Marcus, she would do so as his equal. Playing the distressed damsel did not sit well with her. She would find alternative lodgings even if she had to crawl to the village on her hands and knees through a muddy swamp.

"The air will do me good. And I will be safe enough if I ride."

"*Non*, *madame*." Selene looked horrified. "I will take the cart and come with you. There are things I need, so it will not be a wasted journey."

Anna gave the woman a warm smile. "Thank you, Selene."

"I will bring the tonic to your room and meet you in the courtyard in twenty minutes."

"I'll just get my cape."

Anna went into the chapter house and found her cape draped over the chair. Everything about the room reminded her of Marcus. A musky masculine scent hung in the air, the potent smell rousing memories of his bronze skin and muscular chest. She could almost hear his rich drawl, the sweet curses that fell from his lips as he moved inside her.

As she scanned the room, she realised she would miss being at the monastery with him. She would miss watching him eat and sleep, miss the seductive smile that promised a wealth of pleasure at his hands.

Why did life always bring such bitter disappointment?

Her gaze fell to the ink pot on his desk. On her return from the village, she would sit and write to Miss Beaufort. She would apologise; she would explain the circumstances surrounding Marcus Danbury's betrayal.

Anna was still standing in quiet contemplation when Selene walked past carrying a tray.

"I'm in here, Selene."

She stopped and came into the room. Her gaze fell to the cape over Anna's arm, and she caught a brief flash of disapproval in the woman's dark brown eyes. "Here, you must drink this," she said, balancing the tray on the edge of the desk. "It is valerian tea. It is known to help with stomach spasms."

"If it works, I shall be forever in your debt." Anna offered a chuckle in an attempt to distract from the pain. Although after the success with the balm, she was confident in the woman's abilities.

The rich amber liquid smelt of pine and a sticky sort of

sweetness Anna couldn't quite place. After taking a sip of the slightly cloudy drink, she decided she could definitely note pine, and sandalwood, and perhaps clove. Overall, it tasted unpleasant, so she swallowed it down quickly, took a large spoonful of Selene's tonic to cleanse her palate.

"Oh, you can always tell when something is medicinal by the revolting taste." Anna blinked and shook her head vigorously as the liquid trickled down her throat.

"The tea can be bitter, but it will help with the pain." Selene picked up the tray. "I'll take this to the kitchen and then go and get the cart. I do not want Andre to see me. He will demand to go in my place."

Anna was tired of men thinking they had a right to take control of every situation. "Well, I won't tell him. I can wait down by the gate if it helps?"

Selene smiled. "Yes. I will meet you there in twenty minutes."

Stuffing the notes down between her chemise and stays, and grabbing the few French francs she had, Anna wrapped her cape around her shoulders and hurried down to the gate. She wanted to be gone before Marcus returned. Come the evening she would have a new place to stay. The freedom that came with independence would empower her to take a more logical view of her relationship with him. And when she came back for the rest of her things, she'd have the strength she needed to talk.

"This is very good of you, Selene," Anna said as she climbed into the cart.

"There is a blanket for your legs," Selene replied, glancing at the woollen object nestled between them on the wooden seat.

"I'm fine. My head still feels hot though the cramps have eased a little." Anna stifled a yawn as they rumbled along the muddy lane. "Forgive me. I don't think I slept for more than a few minutes last night."

"Mr. Danbury said *le troubadour* brought many to the inn

last night."

"I have never seen so many people packed into such a small space. But it's good for business, good for Lenard."

The rhythmical rocking made Anna feel nauseous, and she held onto the seat.

"You seem to like it in the village," Selene said, gazing ahead.

Anna nodded. "The people are friendly, and it makes a change from the bustling streets of London." In truth, anywhere was preferable to Labelles.

"You do not miss your home?" Selene cast a sidelong glance. "You do not long to be back there?"

"I miss it a little." She did not miss London at all and had no desire to return. She had always hoped to go home to Marlow but, in reality, the excitement she used to feel burning in her belly had gone. "In all honesty, I have felt more at home here than anywhere else my entire life."

"So you intend to stay?"

Anna shrugged. "No one knows what the future holds. No one knows—"

She stopped abruptly. Her head felt light and dizzy, and she struggled to focus on the road ahead. Tiny lights crackled and sparked to hinder her vision, and she could feel herself falling.

"Are you well, *madame*?"

"I … I'm not sure. Could you stop the cart for a moment?"

The cart rattled to a halt, and Selene turned to face her. "Is it the pain? Are you too hot?"

Anna found it hard to absorb the woman's words. It felt as though she was being pulled back from reality. Everything grew misty, a little hazy.

"Would you like to lie down?" It took a moment for Selene's mumbling to penetrate her addled brain.

Anna heard the words *cart* and *blanket.*

Then she heard nothing as she descended into a dark abyss.

CHAPTER 19

Marcus stormed through the nave. The brisk ride had done nothing to help soothe his troubled conscience. He had been down to the village in the hope of retrieving the letter. The letter he should never have written. The letter he should never have sent.

But he was too late.

On the ride back he'd ventured down to the shore, thought it best to stay away from the monastery and so spent a few hours pondering the strange emotions plaguing his mind and body whenever he thought of Anna Sinclair. He contemplated the consequences of informing Coombes he'd made a mistake about the smugglers' intention to transport contraband. He couldn't do it, of course. Conspiring with criminals against the Crown was considered to be on par with the *owlers* smuggling their wool to France through Romney Marsh. Indeed, Marcus had no desire to turn traitor or wrestle with the hangman's noose.

"Mr. Danbury. Mr. Danbury." Selene came running through the cloisters, tendrils of hair falling around her face, her eyes wide and fearful. "Thank goodness you are back. I have been waiting for hours."

Marcus raced towards her, taking hold of her arms before she fell to the floor in a breathless heap. "What is it? Is something wrong?"

The wild look in the woman's eyes caused a frisson of fear to shoot through him.

"I … I don't know." She shook her head, closed her eyes as though desperate to rid her mind of a terrible memory.

"Just stop for a minute," Marcus instructed. "Try to calm yourself."

Selene sucked in a breath and then suddenly flew into his arms, pressing her cheek to his chest. Marcus froze, not knowing what to do or how to react. He patted her arm and offered a few words of comfort before forcing her to straighten.

"Has someone been here?" he demanded. What the hell was the matter with the woman? "Has someone been hurt?"

"It is Miss Sinclair," Selene blurted.

Marcus almost crumpled to the floor, too, as panic gripped him by the throat and threatened to crush his airways. "Miss Sinclair? What's happened? Where is she?"

Selene shook her head. "That is just it. I do not know."

"You don't know? You're not making any sense." He considered grabbing her and shaking the words from her mouth. However, experience forced him to modify his tone. "Has something happened to Miss Sinclair?" he repeated.

Perhaps Anna had packed her things and left the monastery. Perhaps the fear that was currently clawing away at his heart was unfounded.

"I … I took Miss Sinclair to the village," Selene began with a sniffle. "She was not well. She was suffering from a headache, fever, and became—how you say—delirious."

Marcus felt the blood drain from his face, run the length of his body to pool at his feet. His last words to her were said in anger. Out of guilt and frustration he had suggested she leave.

"Where is she now?"

"That is the problem. I do not know."

Marcus' frantic gaze scanned the garth and the ancient corridor, glanced behind to the nave and the chapel. Was there anyone about who could tell him what the bloody hell was going on?

Draping an arm around his cook, he led her into the chapter house, made her sit and take a nip of brandy. It took a tremendous amount of effort not to charge out into the courtyard, mount his horse and gallop down to the village. But he knew that a few minutes spent procuring information would save time in the end.

"You took Miss Sinclair to the village," he repeated in as calm a tone as he could muster as he perched on the edge of his desk. "What time was this?"

Selene shrugged. "I don't know. I think sometime after one."

"But that was hours ago."

"*Oui*. I have been here, waiting for you to return."

"Did you not alert Andre? Ask him to come and find me?"

"I did not think you would want me to mention it until you knew what to do."

Marcus suppressed his frustration. In truth, he was annoyed with himself for staying out so long. "What happened then?"

Selene nodded. "I took her in the cart. She wanted to lie down, but found she could not stay awake, and so I covered her with a blanket. I … I left her for a minute while I ran to get help. But when I came back she had gone."

"Gone? Gone!" People did not just disappear. "Perhaps one of the villagers saw her and offered assistance. Perhaps she wandered to a house, and they took her in."

"*Non!*" Selene cried. "I could not wake her."

Marcus stood up. "She had lost consciousness?"

"Miss Sinclair felt sleepy. She closed her eyes, and I could not rouse her." Selene held her head in her hands and sniffed again. "What if she had lost her way and cannot remember where to go? What if I was wrong and she did speak to a man in the stables that night, and he has taken her somewhere far away?"

Guilt stabbed at his chest as a way of punishing him. He had made her ill. His unforgivable actions had brought her nothing but torment and distress.

"I'm sure all will be well," he lied, hoping Selene's dramatic account did not paint an accurate picture of events. What if Victor did have an accomplice staying in the village and he'd witnessed Anna's vulnerable state? Then another thought entered his mind. "I shall go down to the village and search for her. But before I go, I want to ask you something."

Her head shot up, her brown eyes growing wide. "What is it?"

"On the night Miss Sinclair spoke with the intruder, she said she saw you wandering the corridors. She said you ran out through the nave." It wasn't a lie, just a slight manipulation of the truth. "What were you doing?"

Selene gasped as her hand fluttered to her chest. "She … she was mistaken. Andre woke me when you asked him to search our rooms. If you ask him, he will tell you."

Marcus didn't know what the hell to believe anymore. He didn't want to believe any of his staff would conspire to deceive him.

"Very well." He sighed, brushing his hand through his hair. "Tell Andre I am going down to the village. Tell him to meet me there promptly, that I shall need his assistance."

Without another word Marcus strode out to the stables. He rode to the village in less than ten minutes, dismounting and tethering his horse before surveying the quiet street. One or two people were milling about, and he noticed Selene's father, Pierre Lessard, scurrying along towards him.

"*Pardon*, Monsieur Lessard." Marcus waved his hand to get the elderly man's attention, rushed over to block his path. "Have you seen Miss Sinclair today? She came down to the village a few hours ago with Selene. They were travelling in the cart."

Being petite in stature, Monsieur Lessard craned his neck, pushed his thinning hair from his brow as he shook his head. "*Non*. Not today. But Madame Lessard has been ill, and I've been occupied for most of the day."

"Is Samuel at home?"

"Samuel?" The man looked puzzled. "He is in Lyon though you are not the only person to mention him to me these last few days."

It occurred to Marcus that Antoine Tullier had made a mistake. Surely, Samuel's father would be the first to know of his return home. But then Marcus thought of his own father, of how he would sell his soul to avoid being in his company, and so it all seemed more plausible.

"Someone told me Samuel was in the inn last night."

"*Oui, oui*. So I hear. But why would he travel all the way from Lyon and not visit his mother?" Monsieur Lessard gave a decisive nod. "*Non*. There must be some mistake."

"Perhaps you're right," Marcus said with a sigh as he did not wish to worry the man. He pulled his watch from his pocket and checked the time before replacing it. "Lenard will be open for business. I'll go and speak to him."

Marcus inclined his head and stepped aside so Monsieur Lessard could continue on his journey. He was about to enter the inn when he saw Andre hurtling towards him in the cart. Marcus had expected the man to come alone but noticed both Selene and Justin perched on the wooden seat.

They jumped from the cart and rushed over to him.

"What do you need me to do?" Andre asked. Before Marcus could pass comment, Andre jerked his head to his companions. "They wanted to come. I thought we could search a larger area if there were more of us."

Marcus nodded. "I'll speak to Lenard. You check with the

shopkeepers. Talk to anyone who might have been passing." He turned to Selene. "Is your brother still in Lyon?" He was deliberately abrupt to throw her off guard.

Selene appeared confused. "Samuel? Yes, I assume he is. My parents have not mentioned they're expecting him home."

"Very well," he said, raising his chin in resignation. "We'll meet back here in ten minutes and then decide what to do once we've examined any new information."

They all went their separate ways, and Marcus marched into the inn. Lenard was standing behind the worn oak counter, wiping tankards with a cloth. Besides the minstrel sitting at the table next to the fire, the inn was empty.

"Monsieur Danbury," Lenard said as he continued to clean the vessel. "Is it not a little early for you?"

Marcus found it somewhat awkward being polite to a man involved in nefarious activities. Indeed, he had not dismissed the prospect that the smugglers had grown suspicious of his interest in their movements and so had sought to hold Miss Sinclair for ransom.

"I am looking for Miss Sinclair. She came down to the village a few hours ago with Selene and disappeared."

"Disappeared?" he repeated placing the tankard and cloth on the counter and giving Marcus his full attention. "But you said she came with Selene. Surely she knows of her whereabouts?"

"No. Selene left her for a moment and when she returned Miss Sinclair had gone. The lady is ill, and I fear she may not be capable of returning home without assistance." Marcus spoke casually, calmly, yet inside his heart raced so fast he feared it might burst from his chest.

Lenard untied the white apron hanging around his waist. "Then I shall come with you and help you look for her. If she's wandered into the woods, you'll struggle to find her on your own."

Marcus was surprised by the man's concern and offer of

help. It raised doubts about the smugglers' involvement. Guilt flared once again. He would have to find a way to reveal what he knew awaited the smugglers should they set sail in the hope of reaching England.

"Jacob," Lenard shouted to the minstrel sitting by the fire. He threw the garment, and the man caught it. "Keep watch while I'm gone."

The minstrel looked a little baffled, but he nodded and set about putting on the apron before they'd opened the door.

They met Andre, Justin and Selene outside.

"No one has seen Miss Sinclair today," Andre said solemnly. "We have asked in every shop, stopped people walking by."

"Perhaps she wandered away, got lost and took shelter somewhere?" Lenard offered. "You said she was ill and so could not have gone far."

Marcus tried to think logically but with every passing minute the fear of never seeing Anna again, of living with the fact something tragic had happened to her, became increasingly unbearable.

Think, think, he told himself. Had he been alone he would have thumped his head to jostle his languid brain into action.

Logically, there were only two options. Anna, feeling delirious and disoriented as a result of her sudden illness, had made an attempt to walk back to the monastery. Or Victor's accomplice had followed the cart to the village and abducted her with the intention of doing her harm. Despite his experience with the depraved depths of the criminal mind, the thought of the comte having a mysterious partner, one prepared to loiter in a quiet village for three weeks in the hope of stealing Anna away, seemed too far-fetched.

"I think we should assume she has tried to make her way home," Marcus said with an air of confidence. "She could not have followed the lane back else one of us would have seen her on our way here."

"What about the woods?" Lenard said. "It seems a logical place to start."

"Agreed," Marcus said. "We'll stay together for a few minutes and let our instincts guide us." It was a method he had used before, a method that rarely failed him.

They headed out of the village, past the row of yellow stone buildings, past the old oak tree that had stood watch for more than two hundred years. There was only one path leading into the woods, and so they walked for a few minutes through the lush green vegetation, calling out to Anna, tapping at the undergrowth with a long stick they'd found discarded.

They all stopped when the track branched in opposite directions.

"There is an old cottage down there," Lenard said, pointing to the right. "Perhaps she's taken shelter."

Marcus narrowed his gaze. Lenard was referring to the cottage used by the smugglers to store their goods. The same smugglers Marcus had seen behind Lenard's inn retrieving items from his cellar.

"We'll take the path to the right," Marcus said, gesturing to Lenard. It would give him an ideal opportunity to advise the innkeeper against immoral pastimes. He nodded to Andre. "You and Justin go left. Call out if you find her."

"What about me?" Selene asked. "Can I come with you to search the cottage?"

As the last person to see Anna, Marcus wanted to keep Selene close. And this business with Samuel Lessard still bothered him. "Very well."

"How far do you want us to go?" Andre asked.

"Walk for a mile or so and then head back this way. When we've searched the cottage, we'll head to the shore. There are a few caves along the coastline that might be worth checking."

Marcus observed Lenard's reaction to his suggestion. The innkeeper's expression remained impassive. There were many logical reasons why one would not dare to climb slippery rocks and venture into a cave. But Lenard offered no such protest. It was all rather puzzling.

It took five minutes to reach the cottage. Selene waited outside while Marcus and Lenard searched the dilapidated building.

Everything was as Marcus had left it a few nights earlier. The memory roused images of Anna. That night he had stood in the cottage struggling to concentrate on his mission. Indeed, their clumsy coupling in the cave brought a smile to his lips, despite the feeling of anguish he was trying to keep at bay.

When he found her, he would ask for her forgiveness. It would take time for her to trust him again and so he would just have to be patient.

"The place is empty." Lenard sighed.

They stood together in the main living area.

"We'll walk down to the cliff edge and check around there." Marcus decided this was probably the best opportunity he'd have for a private discussion. "I hear your daughter is ill?"

For the first time in the last hour, Lenard's expression grew solemn. "The doctor says he needs more money. He says she may never walk again."

Marcus felt a sudden burst of compassion. "I trust you do not have the funds to cover the doctor's expenses?"

Lenard appeared surprised by the impertinent comment. "I have not made my private affairs known to anyone," he said defensively. "What makes you think it would be a problem?"

Marcus put his hand on the man's shoulder. It was a gesture of friendship, a way to lessen the blow when he challenged him over his late night activities. "I heard you've been keeping bad company. That you're moving spirits from your cellar."

Lenard swallowed visibly. "Spirits? Why would I do such a thing?"

"Please don't lie to me," Marcus implored. "I am trying to

help you. You have moved liquor from your cellar, have you not?"

There was a brief moment of silence.

"*Oui*." Panic flashed in Lenard's eyes. "But please do not tell anyone. Two men approached me and offered to buy bottles of liquor, wanted to store other items in my cellar." He threw his hands in the air. "What was I to do? I needed a large sum of money and could not wait the months it would take to sell the same quantity at the inn."

It crossed Marcus' mind to ask why he'd not sought help from his friends, but he understood Lenard was a proud man.

"You know the smugglers will not make it past Guernsey. The revenue ship will be waiting to intercept them. The men who approached you, were they French?"

"One French, one English, and they spoke of another man though I never met him." Lenard threw his hands up. "Please, I cannot say any more. If they knew I had said anything, well, …"

Marcus dropped his hand. "And that is the extent of your involvement?"

Lenard nodded frantically. "*Oui*. I should never have accepted their offer."

The man looked terrified, and Marcus was relieved to find, that in alerting Coombes, he had not betrayed any of the villagers. "I doubt the men from the Custom House will care where the contraband came from. Their only interest lies in the men unwilling to pay duty to the Crown. But if ever a similar opportunity presents itself, I strongly suggest you refuse."

Lenard nodded.

"Just one more question," Marcus continued. "Have you seen Samuel Lessard in the last few days? I ask because I thought I saw him in the inn on the night the minstrel played. But both Selene and her father insist he is in Lyon."

"That is strange," Lenard said, scratching his head. "I thought I saw him, too. He never spoke, and someone else must have served him, but I am sure I recognised him amongst the crowd."

"I think I need to question Selene again."

Marcus held the cottage door open for Lenard. They stepped outside and scanned the deserted area looking for his cook.

"Perhaps she has wandered around to the back of the house," Lenard said, noting his concerned expression.

"Trust me." Marcus was suddenly feeling far more perceptive than he had in days. "Selene obviously had an ulterior motive for coming with us. Don't ask me why, but I believe if we find Selene we will also find Miss Sinclair."

CHAPTER 20

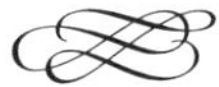

She was dead!

Well, that was the first thought to enter Anna's head when she opened her eyes. But she would have expected the fiery pits of hell to be a lot less cold and dank. The floor beneath her felt damp and moist. A fine trace of soil stuck to her palms as she lay patting the solid surface. In a panic she tried to sit up, expecting to hit her head on the lid of the coffin, expecting to be overwhelmed by a sudden fear of suffocating. But there was no lid or wooden box to restrict her movements.

Inhaling deeply, she struggled to focus in the darkness. All about her seemed to sway. Black shapes danced before her eyes, moving closer and then pulling away. The throbbing ache in her temples did not help matters, and when she tried to stand she clutched at nothing in the hope of finding hidden support in the depths of the shadows.

What in heaven's name had happened to her?

She remembered sitting in the cart on the way to the village. She remembered chatting to Selene, remembered the horrified look on the woman's face as her world became a hazy blur.

So how had she ended up all alone, curled up on the dirty floor?

As her eyes became accustomed to her surroundings, she realised she was standing in the middle of a room. Amidst the gloom, she could just make out the outline of a door, and with her hands held out in front of her to guide her way, she shuffled blindly forward.

The solid wooden door had been reinforced with metal strips. Despite running her hands over every inch of the grooved panels, she found no handle, no key in the lock. Anna pushed it, hit out, kicked it until her toes were sore and she felt dizzy.

"Help!" she shouted numerous times. Too many to count. "Can anyone hear me?"

But each time she was met with an eerie stillness.

With her vision restricted, all other senses were more attuned. The faint rhythmical swooshing sound made her think of the sea, like undulating waves crashing against a rocky shore. Indeed, mingled with the rather repugnant earthy smell, she noted a hint of salt in the air.

So, she was in a building near the sea.

Perhaps the smugglers were aware of Marcus' assignment and had taken her hostage in a bid to secure his silence. But he had already alerted Coombes of their plans, although they probably didn't know that. And while Lenard needed money to help his daughter, she could not believe him capable of such deception and cruelty. Perhaps Victor's accomplice had progressed from anonymous threats in the stables to kidnap and murder. Of course, he'd not have the stomach to commit the act himself and had locked her up in a tomb in the hope she'd suffocate.

The last thought caused panic to flare.

It was a tomb!

She swung around, tapped the wall to her left and followed it until her fingers found the powdery indentations carved into the stone.

With her airways closing, she gasped a breath as she stumbled back into the middle of the room. Just the thought of sharing such a small enclosed space with heaven knows how many corpses was alarming in itself.

Corpses!

Anna shuddered, stamped her feet and wriggled in disgust as though she had walked into a giant cobweb and feared an equally large spider had crawled beneath her cape.

The frantic movements made her feel lightheaded again, and she sagged to the floor to calm her ragged breathing and racing heart.

Was this to be how she would meet her demise?

Was she to take her last breath all alone in a tomb?

Then another thought hit her, the blow more painful than anything she'd ever felt before. Her last words to Marcus had been said in spite and anger. He would never know how much she cared for him. He would never know that her time with him at the monastery had been the most wonderful experience of her entire life. She wanted to tell him she loved him; she understood his pain, could forgive him for his betrayal.

With no concept of time, Anna wasn't sure how long she'd sat there contemplating her fate, replaying the turbulent events leading her to this precarious point in her life. She imagined Victor's evil grin of satisfaction, a glint of pleasure flashing in his cold, black eyes; she heard her father's solemn warning that all sinners must repent or pay a hefty price.

Indeed, with her thoughts just as chaotic as the night she'd heard the intruder in the monastery, she almost missed the sound of footsteps outside.

Jumping to her feet, she rushed forward. "Help. Can you hear me?" She thumped on the door with clenched fists.

It was probably an animal or a group of children playing nearby. No doubt, they'll have scampered home to tell their parents they'd heard the terrifying wail of a ghost from inside a tomb.

The sudden clinking of a key in the lock captured her attention, and she stepped back into the darkness. The door creaked open, beams of light piercing the shadows. A figure filled the doorway: his outline revealing a tall scrawny frame.

He stepped inside and then came to an abrupt halt. "*Ce que l'enfer? Qui es-tu*?"

Anna swallowed down her nerves. "What do you mean, who am I?" Now the door was open perhaps she could get away. "Surely you're the one who locked me in this morbid place."

The mysterious silhouette took a few steps closer. After scanning her face, his eyes widened as he muttered a foul curse. "What are you doing in here?"

Recognising him as Samuel Lessard, the man they'd seen smoking his clay pipe whilst listening to the minstrel, she said, "Well, you're the one with the key. What possible reason could I have for being in a …" She glanced around the small, compact space. The rows of stone memorial plaques lining the walls were visible now. "In a mausoleum?"

He stepped closer, his brows meeting in the middle as his beady gaze drifted over her. "Ah, it is the whore from England. Poor Marie, left all alone with a pile of rotting corpses."

Anna shivered. Samuel Lessard was the man who had spoken to her in the stables. It was uncanny how he sounded so much like Victor. Yet there was one distinct difference. This man's words lacked conviction. When Victor spoke, everyone stopped and took notice.

"Who told you my name?" she said, finding the courage to raise her chin.

"Ah, you do not deny your profession, yet challenge me over such a simple thing." He looked beyond her shoulder to a roll of linen lying on top of old sacking on the floor near the far wall. Offering a relieved sigh, he said, "I shall ask you again. How did you get in here? Did those blackguards hope to swindle me? Did they ask you to steal the key from Selene?"

Despite her curiosity, Anna ignored the comment about swindling blackguards. "Selene has a key?"

Samuel Lessard waved his hand in the air. "But of course, this tomb belongs to our family."

What motive could Selene have for locking her in the chamber? But then she *had* been with Selene when she was taken ill. Her thoughts drifted back to the valerian tea—although she had hardly drunk enough of the disgusting liquid to render her unconscious. Unless it had something to do with the tonic she'd swallowed? Anna snorted. As the cook, Selene could have been slowly poisoning her for days.

But why?

"It may well belong to your family," Anna began, glaring at him with contempt, "but I doubt you've come here to pay your respects."

He smirked. "Even the dead have their uses. My ancestors have been kind enough to keep watch on an item I have stored in here. And have provided shelter for me these last few nights."

Anna did not need to follow his gaze to know he meant the roll of material lying on the floor behind her. "I'm surprised you went to so much trouble for a roll of linen."

"Linen? *Non, non!* Are the beautiful wings of a butterfly not hidden in the depths of the caterpillar's bland cocoon?"

It took a moment for her to comprehend his meaning, but then it occurred to her that the linen protected something infinitely more precious.

"You mean the roll contains silk."

He raised an amused brow and nodded.

"I assume you're not planning to take up dressmaking? I know of no maiden who desires to smell of salt and decomposing flesh."

"Now I understand how you have managed to acquire so

much money," he said with a chuckle. "It seems gentlemen pay handsomely for a witty tongue." Tapping his chest, he added, "I must thank you, Marie, for funding my expedition."

The man spoke in riddles.

As though sensing her confusion, he said, "If you want to keep your money safe, you should not hide it under the bed."

It took every ounce of willpower Anna possessed not to shove her hand down between her chemise and stays to check her notes were still there. With a bundle lying on each breast, she could feel them when she moved. But she had not counted it for weeks.

"Didn't anyone ever tell you, you should repent your sins?" She was starting to sound like her father. "That if you don't, they will come back to haunt you."

He gave a mocking jeer, held his hands together in prayer. "*Pardonne-moi!* I ask for forgiveness. But you should be grateful I did not steal it all." With a heavy sigh, he pointed to the roll of silk encased in linen. "As much as I am enjoying your repartee, in an hour or two the sun will be setting, and I fear I must be on my way. If you will be so kind as to hand me my goods."

Anna almost told him to go to the devil, but she supposed she should be grateful he had opened the door else she could well have suffocated in the confined space. Suppressing her ire, she bent down and gathered the roll up into her arms.

"Take it," she said, suppressing the need to throw it at him as he scooped it out of her grasp. "I hope the expedition I've funded proves fruitful."

He shrugged. "Fifty of your English pounds will get me to your shore, pay for my keep, for the odd turn at the tables." He thrust the roll under his arm. "Now, it is time for me to be on my way."

Anna followed him towards the door, relieved to feel fresh

air breezing over her face. "I'm sure I shall know the moment a lady enters a room wearing a dress made from that silk."

"I doubt it." He turned and scanned the tomb. "Had I known this was to be your fate I would have asked Selene to steal it all. What good is having money hidden under the bed when you shall perish in here?"

Anna gulped and shook her head. "But surely you mean to let me leave?"

"Ah, *non*. It is not possible. Not now you know of my plans, know of my silk."

Taking a deep breath for courage, Anna blurted, "I am leaving this tomb whether you to try to stop me or not."

Samuel Lessard tutted. "Why must everything be so difficult?" he said wearily. "Do not make me draw my knife. Do not —" His attention shifted, and he raised his chin as wrinkles formed on his brow. Anna thought she'd heard something, too. But then, with a quick shake of the head he stared at her. "Where were we?"

With the door still open, this was her only chance to escape.

Without giving the matter another thought, she charged towards him, barging past in a desperate bid to be far away from the hideous place.

The mausoleum stood on the edge of a cliff leading down to the sea. The few gravestones dotted about gave the impression that all others had fallen to the rocky shore as the battering waves eroded the earth, sucking it away. She had no option but to run straight ahead and managed to take a few strides before being knocked to the ground, her face hitting the pebbled pathway.

Rolling onto her back, she met Samuel Lessard's irritated glare as he loomed over her, wielding the roll of material like a floppy sword.

"Get up. Get up," he repeated, his tone revealing irritation as opposed to anger.

"Samuel. Samuel." The feminine cry drifted through the air. Anna glanced to her left to see Selene running towards them, scraping back the ebony locks clinging to her face. She stopped at Anna's side and put her hand on her chest as she tried to catch her breath. "What … what have you done?"

Samuel Lessard broke into a torrent of abusive curses, speaking so quickly in his native tongue Anna struggled to make sense of it.

"Just go, Samuel. I shall take care of Miss Sinclair." Selene flicked her fingers to shoo him away.

Samuel cursed again. "What, so you may tell the whole village I locked her in a tomb?"

"It does not matter. Just go now before the others come." Selene was gabbling her words in a desperate bid to be rid of him. "The boat will be leaving soon. You must go."

If Samuel left now, Anna might never discover the truth. Why had Selene locked her inside the tomb? Why had she stolen her money? How had Samuel discovered her name and previous profession?

"So, you *are* to blame, Monsieur Lessard. Mr. Danbury will not let you leave when he discovers you were the one who poisoned me and locked me in that tomb. He will be here soon."

Fear flashed in the skinny man's eyes. "I … I must leave tonight. I cannot stay here. It is not safe for me." His gaze darted to Selene. "Just tell her, Selene. Tell her it was you."

Selene's mouth hung open, and she snapped it shut. "Liar! Do not lie to protect yourself, Samuel."

Samuel Lessard shook his head. He bent down, offered his hand and helped her to her feet. "Selene wanted to scare you, to—"

"Liar!" Selene yelled, flying at her brother, punching and kicking him. He pushed her away, and she fell back, her arms flailing.

"Selene found your hidden money. She knew I had to leave

here before my friends from Lyon came looking for me. And so, yes, she gave me your fifty pounds and in return begged me to hide in the stables and frighten you."

Frighten me?

All Anna could do was stand in stupefied silence and shake her head. What possible reason could Selene have for wanting to scare her? A few seconds felt like hours as a range of emotions flooded her chest: anger, confusion, relief. She sighed. Victor was dead. And she did not need to live in fear of an accomplice hiding in the village.

"Why?" The solitary word fell from Anna's lips though it conveyed sorrow and disappointment.

"You do not understand." Selene scrambled to her feet. "It was not meant to be like this."

"No. You intended to leave me in that godforsaken place." Anna thrust her finger towards the mausoleum. "I would have been dead come morning. Is that what you wanted?"

Selene sniffed. "*Non! Non!* I would have come back when it was dark. Then you would not have known it was me."

"Why?" Anna repeated. "I have been kind to you. I have tried to be helpful, useful with the chores."

Selene held her head in her hands and sobbed. "I could not help it. You were taking him away from me. I … I just wanted you to go far from here, to go home."

Samuel cursed at his sister, spitting each word as a snake would venom.

Taking him away? Did she mean Marcus?

"How did you know I'd used the name Marie?" Anna did not wish to repeat what Samuel Lessard had said about her being a whore.

"I heard you talking, read about it in a letter."

Anna gasped. "You read Mr. Danbury's private correspondence?"

“I did not have a choice. I needed to know who you were … to know of your intentions.”

“You could have spoken to me. You could have made your feelings known. But instead, you poisoned me, stole from me, tried to—”

Anna stopped abruptly. The sound of someone calling her name caught her attention. Four figures came charging out from the woods. Anna’s heart soared when she noticed Marcus leading the group of men.

With an ear-piercing shriek from Selene and another blasphemous curse from Samuel, both brother and sister turned and fled, racing down the path towards the shore.

CHAPTER 21

"Anna!"

Marcus ignored the two frantic figures fleeing the scene. He could not tear his gaze away from the heavenly vision before him. Breaking into a run, he charged ahead. An overwhelming sense of relief consumed him, all the pain, fear and distress melting away.

Anna was safe and well.

He called out to her again—a cry of anguish to express the desperate need for her clawing away inside. She ran into his open arms, and he swung her around, hugged her tight until they struggled to breathe.

"I thought I'd lost you," he said, lowering her down until her feet touched the ground. Blissfully ignorant to those looking on, he took her face between his palms and kissed her deeply. "I'm sorry for writing the blasted letter. I'm sorry for suggesting you should leave."

"It doesn't matter now." She threw her arms around his neck, ran her fingers through his hair.

"What happened to you?" he asked, stepping back and holding her hands as his eyes devoured every inch of her, searching for any sign of illness or injury. "Selene said you felt dizzy, that she came back to the cart but you'd gone. Did someone lure you away? Was it Samuel Lessard?"

Anna shook her head. "Selene locked me in the mausoleum. But I'll explain it all later. You must go after her. She is not thinking clearly. I fear she could do herself harm."

Andre cleared his throat. "*Pardon*. But we will go and find Selene."

Marcus inclined his head and without another word, Andre, Lenard and Justin hurried off in pursuit of his cook.

Anna dropped her arms. "You should go with them."

"I'm not leaving you."

"Then I'll follow."

Marcus stroked her face, brushed the tendrils of golden hair away gently, and took her hand. "We'll go together."

They hurried down the steep, rocky path leading from the cliff edge to the sandy shore. With the tide low, the beach appeared to stretch for half a mile or more, and Marcus noticed a solitary figure sprinting towards the sea.

"It's Samuel Lessard," Anna said, following his gaze as they hurried along the coastline in a bid to catch up with the men and Selene. "The package under his arm is a roll of silk. He intends to set sail in an attempt to smuggle it into England. But surely he's not going to run into the sea with it. Doesn't he know the salt water will ruin it?"

Marcus had noted the sailing vessel on the horizon. There would be a small boat waiting to ferry Lessard across. "They need to move now. When the tide is low, they're less likely to be seen as they're further away from the shore. When the tide is high, there's a greater risk of them crashing onto the rocks as the water surges and swells and can be unpredictable."

"I can see a small boat," she said.

Marcus glanced up at the thick granite-coloured cloud drifting closer to the shore. "No doubt he means to reach the boat before the storm breaks. It's possible the other smugglers have already boarded with their liquor, tobacco and tea. Lenard told me he sold liquor to the smugglers. I imagine from the quantity we found in the cave some of it is stolen, too."

"Lenard confessed?" He felt Anna's penetrative gaze, heard the surprise in her tone.

"There's not much to confess. He knew of their criminal intentions but needed the money. He never had any plans to smuggle the goods himself."

"Does he know of your involvement?" she asked with a sense of trepidation. "Does he know you're the informer?"

"No. But he knows I understand the risks involved, and I've warned him to avoid similar ventures in the future."

Anna gripped his hand. "I've a lot to tell you. But first, we must make sure Selene is safe."

Marcus' heart swelled with pride at her compassion for Selene. The woman had caused an immense amount of trouble and still he had no idea why. Anna's sudden gasp made him focus his attention on the unnerving sight ahead.

"Selene is climbing the rocks," Anna cried. "It's too high, Marcus. She'll never make it up to the cliff edge. What if she falls?"

They could hear Andre shouting Selene to stop. Lenard and Justin remained on the sand while Andre grabbed onto the first rock and hoisted himself up. By the time Marcus and Anna reached them, Selene had climbed five or six and had turned around to look out over the vast expanse of water.

"Do not follow me," Selene shouted balancing precariously as she leant back. The solid lump of stone provided the only support. "I will jump."

Panic flared in Marcus' chest. Despite all she had done, he had lived with her for years. She'd worked hard, been loyal until now. Perhaps she was suffering from some imbalance of the mind? Perhaps she had done the terrible things at the behest of her brother?

"Wait, Selene." Anna let go of his hand and stepped forward. "Let me talk to you. Let me come up as I cannot hear you down here."

Marcus put his hand on her elbow. "No, Anna. As much as I pity the woman, we do not know what she is capable of. I've almost lost you once. I'll not stand here and watch you put your life in danger."

"*Pardon*, *madame*, but I agree," Andre said as he clung to the first rock. "I do not think it is wise."

"No!" Selene cried. "You must stay where you are." Her body appeared stiff, rigid. She had already proved to be unpredictable. One sudden jerk, one wrong step and she'd come crashing all the way down to the bottom. "I have ruined everything with my silly little *fantaisie*."

"It doesn't matter," Anna implored. "We will talk. We will find a way through it all."

Marcus stepped closer and whispered in Anna's ear. "I can't have her back at the monastery. Not after what she has done. Don't make promises I cannot keep."

She turned and gave him a weak smile. "I know."

"I am a thief, a liar, an evil woman," Selene sobbed as she wiped the tears from her face. "I do not want to hang."

"You're not going to hang," Marcus reassured her. "No one will know of it. We all swear to say nothing of the matter. If you come down, we will do as Miss Sinclair suggests. We will find a solution."

He didn't have the heart to tell her that her brother would most probably hang once the revenue ship intercepted the lugger. Unless they had the money to pay the duty for all the goods they carried.

The first few spots of rain began to fall. They were light

enough so one might think they'd imagined feeling the wet drop land on their skin.

"Please, Selene," Anna implored as the drizzle threatened to progress into a downpour. "Come down so we can all go home."

Selene shook her head, her frantic gaze flitting between Anna and Marcus.

"Let Andre help you," Marcus added. "He has always been a true friend to you, and you're making him ill with worry."

"He will not want to be my friend when he learns what I have done."

Andre pulled himself up to the next rock. "I will," he shouted across to her.

"You will all hate me." Selene's fearful gaze locked with Andre's. She shuffled sideways, lost her footing on a loose stone and slid down to the rock below.

"Good God!" Marcus' loud gasp was accompanied by Anna's scream and Andre's French curse.

They all looked on in horror, but then gave a collective sigh of relief when she managed to stand up.

Andre stretched his hand up to her despite being too far away. "Come, Selene. Let me take you home."

With fear in her eyes, Selene pursed her lips and nodded in resignation.

As with any such task, it was always easier to climb up than it was to descend. Numerous times, Selene slipped on the damp rocks, grazing her elbow, tearing the hem of her dress. Amidst all the gasps and sighs and words of encouragement, Andre reached up and offered her his hand. They all sighed again when Andre placed his feet firmly on the ground, and he lowered Selene down to safety.

"*Merci*, Andre. *Merci*," Selene muttered as Andre hugged her. "You have always been good to me, and I did not mean to disappoint you."

Andre whispered to her in French; the words were said too

quietly and quickly for anyone to hear. Selene looked up at him and nodded.

Breaking away from Andre, Selene walked over to Anna and clasped her hands together in prayer. "Forgive me, Miss Sinclair. I should never have given you the tonic. I should never have left you in—" She stopped abruptly and broke into a sob.

"Let's talk about it back at the monastery," Anna said, casting Marcus a nervous glance. "We are all getting wet, and I've not eaten for hours."

Andre stepped forward. "With your permission, Mr. Danbury, I will escort Selene back."

Perhaps all the time he'd spent with Anna had softened his heart. It was impossible to make any decision regarding Selene whilst standing in the wind and rain. "Very well. Be on your way. We will head back to the village to collect my horse and the cart."

Andre nodded, put his arm around Selene and led her away.

"Just a moment," Anna shouted after them. When Selene turned, Anna said, "Do you have my Bible?"

Selene struggled to look their way. "Yes. It is safe."

Anna sighed. "And did you have help to get me into the tomb?"

Marcus knew why she had asked the question. To know the identity of one's enemy brought a level of strength and determination, a level of confidence in one's ability to overthrow them in battle. To be blind and naive brought a constant fear of the unknown.

Selene coughed and cleared her throat. "I said I drove the cart to town, but that was a lie. I came here instead. You were still able to walk a little although your eyes were closed and you were sleepy. There is no one else to blame. Only me."

As Andre led her away, Anna exhaled deeply.

"Are you all right?" Marcus asked, taking her hands in his. They felt soft and warm despite the rain and blustery breeze. "I see you've been using the balm," he added when she only offered a smile.

"Yes," she replied. "Selene is rather adept at making tonics and potions."

Justin and Lenard walked on ahead. Though his coat was damp, Marcus shrugged out of it and draped it over Anna's shoulders.

"Thank you." This time, Anna's smile reached her eyes, and she threaded her arm through his. "Selene is in love with you. That's what all of this has been about."

"In love with me?" Marcus gasped. "Surely not."

Anna hugged his arm. "She thought I would take you away, that she would lose you."

The woman had worked for him for three years, never giving him as much as a second glance. "She never said anything, never gave me the impression she cared."

"Women often keep their feelings hidden. But if one looks closely you will see it in their eyes, in the soft timbre they use when speaking to the object of their affection."

He glanced at her and their gazes locked. He saw it then: love, warmth, and tenderness. The depth of emotion in her eyes touched him.

"But I do not believe Selene truly loves you," she added.

Marcus snorted. "And why is that?"

"When you love someone with all your heart and soul, you do not do things to hurt them." She clung onto him as a sudden gust of wind almost knocked them off their feet. "Heavens, I shall be glad to be indoors."

"Tell me." He stopped and turned to face her. "What do you do when you love someone so deeply?"

She smiled. "You show compassion and understanding, even though you've spent long terrifying hours wondering if you'll live to see the sun rise. You put aside your negative feelings, safe in the knowledge you have something beautiful blossoming in your heart."

Was she telling him she loved him?

Marcus felt his throat constrict. The pain of regret, of never saying the words he knew filled his chest was too much to bear. It suddenly occurred to him that he was scared. Good Lord! He was scared of losing her. He was scared of loving anyone. He was scared of being a constant disappointment.

Fear was his enemy—the only thing standing in the way of true happiness.

As his boots sank into the moist sand, as the wind howled around their ears and the rain pelted their faces, he made the sudden decision to offer her his heart.

"I never meant to betray you," he said, pulling her into an embrace. "I don't give a damn about Miss Beaufort or Dane or some silly cottage in Marlow. I wrote the letter because I care about you. For no other reason than that."

Anna looked up at him and put her hand on his cheek. "I know. A few hours in a tomb full of corpses has taught me to appreciate what truly matters."

"Then I am forgiven?"

She nodded. "You're forgiven."

"If it helps, I shall write a letter of apology to Miss Beaufort. I would not want her to think ill of you when you do not deserve her disdain."

"It is of no consequence. She loves Lord Danesfield. If he's still looking for her after all this time, then he obviously loves her, too. I am confident all will be well."

They were silent for a moment, and he brushed the straggling tendrils from her face.

"And what of us, Anna?" He sounded nothing like himself: the vulnerability in his voice was foreign to him.

She shrugged and offered a coy smile. "I don't know what you mean."

"Are you deliberately trying to make this difficult for me? Is this to be my punishment? To live with the torturous agony that comes with the anticipation of rejection."

Perhaps sensing his fear, knowing he had never been so unguarded with his feelings, she took the first courageous step. "Know this. You are the only man I have ever loved, the only man I would lay down my life for. I will take you any way I can have you, regardless of what you propose."

Marcus swallowed down the hard lump in his throat as he realised his life was worthless without her. "If that is how you feel I propose we marry. I propose we live together in the monastery and farm the land."

A smile touched her lips, and he was not sure if it was a tear trickling down her cheek or a drop of rain. "So, now that I have soft hands again, you want me to start digging in the dirt?"

"I want you any way I can get you—rough, dirty, hot and bothered."

Offering a sultry smirk, she raised a brow and said, "Is that another proposal, Mr. Danbury?"

"No, Miss Sinclair, it's a promise." He pulled her close, devoured her mouth in a kiss that expressed everything he felt in his heart. "I love you, Anna," he said as he broke away.

And then her tears did fall.

EPILOGUE

THREE MONTHS LATER

Anna found Marcus behind the desk in the chapter house. "You rose early this morning."

After waking to find the bed empty, she knew her husband would be eager to finish balancing the ledgers. His current assignment had nothing to do with trailing after smugglers or hiding the mistress of a bawdy house away in an old monastery.

Marcus raised a sinful brow. "Trust me. I had to drag myself away from your warm body. I'm surprised you didn't hear me groan. But I'm eager to ensure the stone walls are reinforced to prevent us losing any more livestock."

Since making the decision to farm the land, Marcus had thrown himself into the project with the same level of passion and determination he did all things. A smile touched her lips when she recalled experiencing the depth of his passion just a few hours earlier.

"I thought you'd be busy scrawling away with pen and ink," she said, noting the letter in his hand, "pushing wooden beads back and forth on that counting device of yours."

"I was, but then I became a little distracted when I realised the letter was from Tristan."

"Tristan!" She could not hide her excitement. "How is he? Was he shocked to hear of our marriage?"

Marcus shook his head. "Not at all. Tristan believes it was a case of love at first sight. Or love at first slap to be more precise. He said he will never forget the look on my face when your palm connected with my cheek."

"Neither will I," she began a little sheepishly. "I never mentioned it before, but I could still see the outline of my fingers on your face an hour later."

"I think you have a fondness for slapping." His mouth curled up into a devilish grin, and when his eyes flashed with desire, the warm feeling in her chest journeyed southward. "From what I remember of last night, my buttocks—"

"Yes, yes," she interjected as her cheeks grew warm, too. "I was there. I do not need you to remind me."

"On second thoughts, perhaps the stone walls can wait." He rubbed his chin as his gaze drifted over her. "Perhaps I did get out of bed too early this morning."

With her heart all aflutter, Anna nodded to the leather wing-back chair. "Then I shall leave you so you may catch an hour's sleep."

"I think we both know I did not have *sleep* in mind."

How could she resist the tempting offer when he spoke with such a rich, languorous drawl? But she chose to use the moment to her advantage, to give her the courage to broach the subject she had been mulling over for days.

"Before we retire to our chamber," she said in as seductive a tone as she could muster, "I would like to discuss another proposal."

Marcus placed the letter on the desk, sat back in the chair and crossed his arms behind his head. "A proposal? Now I am intrigued. Does it involve slapping?"

Anna thrust her hands on her hips. "Be serious for a

moment." She sighed. "When I gave you my great-aunt's brooch—"

"Your great-aunt? You never mentioned it was a genuine family heirloom. I assumed—"

"What? That one of the randy lords bribed me with a gift?"

"Well ... I didn't realise it meant so much to you." He put his hand to his chest. "I find it rather flattering that you chose to give it to me."

"It is of no consequence now as you have given it back to me. But at the time, I thought you needed the money to find another vocation. And you didn't have to agree to take me in, despite the debt you owed to Lord Danesfield."

"You mean you took one look at my relaxed attire and decided I must be debt-ridden."

"Yes. But now I know I was mistaken, and you've smartened up considerably since we've been married." She swallowed deeply. It was best to get it over with. "Now, returning to the matter of my proposal, I would like to take a trip to England."

Marcus shot out of the chair. "England? Why the hell would you want to go back there?"

Anna knew he would not be pleased. "Because I would like to use the money I saved from Labelles and invest it. I would like to open a refuge for women who find themselves alone and with no prospects. I could provide an education. Give them a room until they find employment."

Marcus stared at her, his expression blank, his eyes vacant.

She hoped he would understand. During the few months they had spent together, he had spoken fondly of his mother. But the guilt he had for leaving her to fend for herself still ate away at him.

"If there had been such a place when I came to London, perhaps I would not have met Victor."

"The irony is, had you not met Victor you would never have met me."

He was right, of course. That one horrendous situation had led her straight to Marcus' door.

"I thought you loved it here?" he added. A look of doubt and fear marred his countenance.

"I do, and I would never want to leave permanently. I thought of employing someone to manage the refuge for me. I could interview for the position."

Marcus strode around the desk, pulled her into an embrace and kissed her softly on the mouth. "How can I refuse your request? Had there been such a place for women like my mother then perhaps things would have been different."

Thank heavens.

Anna placed her hand on his chest. Despite his calm tone, his heart was beating hard against her palm. "I know you have so much you want to do here, but Andre and Selene will manage things while you're away."

"You do want me to come with you then?"

He sounded like a little boy lost, and she stood on the tips of her toes to return his tender kiss. "I never want to be without you. Besides, Andre has been looking for an opportunity to prove himself worthy. He is so grateful to us for giving Selene a second chance, and now they plan to marry he could use the extra income."

"It seems you have thought of everything. You do realise my return will be met with a mixed response. Once people discover we are wed, I expect the gossips will claim it to be a great scandal."

Anna smirked. "The illegitimate son of an earl marrying the madam of a bawdy house, why should there be any scandal?"

"You may find it amusing, but people can be cruel."

She had experienced the worst kind of cruelty. Nothing else would ever compare. "Marcus, I don't care what people say about us. We know the truth."

He exhaled deeply. "Very well. Thankfully, you have made my task much easier."

Anna stepped back and frowned. "What task?"

"I, too, was about to propose a short trip to England. Tristan has asked us to visit him in Bedfordshire and I feared you would say no."

"Why didn't you say so before?"

Marcus nodded to the desk. "I've only just opened it. Apparently, he's had a hell of a time of it these last two months and begs for us to come."

"Well," she said with a satisfied sigh. "That's all settled then."

"Not quite. I believe there is the matter of my original proposal to address."

By the lascivious look on his face, Anna did not need to ask what he meant. "You'll have to remind me. With all this talk of England, my mind is a little hazy."

Marcus pulled her into an embrace. He kissed her until her body tingled, delved deep into her mouth until her head felt fuzzy and she was forced to clutch at his shoulders for fear of falling. "Do you remember now? Is your mind any clearer?"

Anna tried to catch her breath. She felt the loss of his hard body as he left her to lock the door. "What … what are you doing?"

Pushing the papers off his desk onto the floor, he settled his hands on her waist and lifted her up to sit on the uncluttered surface. "I am following your advice. When we met, you said one must make the most of any opportunity presented."

"Yes, and I remember you received a slap for your rather salacious reply."

Marcus placed his hands on her ankles, ran them up under her dress and over her bare thighs. "Then I shall make another proposal."

"Yes." The word was accompanied by a soft sigh as his fingers brushed against the spot that ached for his touch.

"I propose you slap me now, as I promise you my salacious intentions will leave you exhausted and incapable of moving a muscle."

Thank you for reading ***What You Propose***.

If you enjoyed this book, please consider leaving a review at the online bookseller of your choice.

~

Discover more about the author at
www.adeleclee.com

~

Turn the page if you would like to read an excerpt from

What You Deserve

Book 3 in the Anything for Love Series.

WHAT YOU DESERVE

BOOK 3 IN THE ANYTHING FOR LOVE SERIES

What if the gentleman who broke your heart is the only one you can turn to for help?

CHAPTER 1

Tristan Wells, seventh Viscount Morford, stood alone in the drawing room of Lord Mottlesborough's townhouse, watching the musicians unpack their instruments in preparation for the concert.

Lady Mottlesborough came scuttling into the room, her hand flying to her chest when she discovered him loitering behind the door. "Good heavens, my lord. You gave me a fright. What on earth are you doing hiding back there?"

Tristan blinked rapidly. Judging by the sight of the excessively large turban wrapped around the matron's head, he should be the one clutching his chest. Beneath the voluminous folds of exotic silk, he imagined she was as bald as the day she was born.

"I am taking a moment to gather my thoughts." Under present circumstances, she could hardly question his motives. While mourning the loss of one's brother rarely affected a gentleman's social calendar, a more subdued countenance was only to be expected.

The lady gave a rueful smile. "I assume your mother has pestered you to leave the house again this evening." She nodded to the musicians and whispered, "I doubt praise for their skill has dragged you here. They are hardly the talk of the Season."

He snorted. "As you are aware, my mother makes no secret of the fact she is keen for me to find a bride."

With Tristan being the only male member of the family, his mother's eagerness for him to produce an heir bordered on desperation.

"I have heard she has a particular lady in mind."

"She has many ladies in mind," Tristan said with a derisive chuckle, "as long as they're from good breeding stock." In truth, he was beginning to feel like a reluctant bull being herded into a field full of heifers.

"I understand your mother's urgency to see you wed," Lady Mottlesborough said. "Despite her mourning period, no one would cast aspersions on the decision to protect one's heritage. Indeed, we are all aware that one's duty and responsibility must come before everything else."

Tristan knew better than anyone the sacrifices one must make for the sake of patrimony. But with his mother still in full mourning, it prevented her from attending functions, and as such, he found it more preferable to wander the corridors of other people's houses than to remain in his own. He also came in hope of finding more stimulating conversation, something that did not involve talk of flounces and other such fripperies.

"For the moment, I have been granted a reprieve," he said with a weary sigh.

Lady Mottlesborough nodded. "And so you linger in the shadows in the hope the ladies won't find you." She raised a curious brow. "Or perhaps it is one particular lady you wish to avoid. Where is the lovely Miss Smythe this evening?"

Miss Priscilla Smythe *was* lovely. She possessed a sweet, kind disposition, a generous heart, and a pretty countenance. Whenever he thought of kissing her, his mind conjured images of summer meadows, birds chirping merrily, and chocolate macaroons. On the whole, he imagined the experience would be pleasant, if not particularly memorable.

"I believe you will find her surrounded by a host of other ladies just as eager to discuss the merits of ribbon over lace."

Lady Mottlesborough nodded despite the hint of contempt in his tone. "I am afraid we ladies tend to take the topic of haberdashery extremely seriously." She chuckled. "Sewing and embroidery are subjects dear to my heart."

Tristan wondered if that's why she wore the turban. Perhaps she carried her frame and threads around with her in case she found the evening's entertainment too dull. "I'm certain that when you stumble upon Miss Smythe, she will be only too happy to hear all about it."

The matron's suspicious gaze drifted over his face. "Perhaps your interest lies elsewhere. Perhaps you have another lady in mind."

Tristan knew to have a care. Friendly overtures were often used to drag snippets of gossip from unsuspecting fools. Many unwilling parties had been forced into an arrangement simply to stop loose tongues from wagging.

"This evening, I am only interested in listening to a soothing melody whilst enjoying my freedom for a little while longer."

He wanted to say that he had no interest in titles or land. He had no interest in the begetting of an heir, or to be the husband of a woman who failed to ignite even the smallest spark of passion in his chest.

Lady Mottlesborough winced at the sound of the harsh chords being struck as the musicians warmed up their bows. "I hate to be the one to ruin an evening, but the Baxendale Quartet are quite mediocre when it comes to Haydn."

"Then I thank you for the warning," he said with a smirk, "and shall take care to sit near the back."

"A splendid idea. Had I not been the hostess, I most certainly would have joined you." Lady Mottlesborough's attention drifted to the door. "And now it seems your plan to go unnoticed has been foiled, my lord."

Tristan followed her gaze to see Miss Priscilla Smythe and her companion, Miss Hamilton, enter the drawing room.

Lady Mottlesborough tapped his arm with her closed fan.

“I’m afraid there is no escaping now,” she said before turning to greet the other guests pouring in through the door.

He suppressed a groan as both ladies smiled sweetly and came over to join him.

“I simply knew we would find you in here, eager to secure the best seat.” Miss Smythe chuckled sweetly, her golden ringlets bobbing up and down in response. She turned to Miss Hamilton. “Lady Morford said he simply adores Haydn.”

“You all know me only too well,” he said, his affable tone bringing on a bout of nausea. In reality, none of them knew him at all.

Tristan sighed inwardly. It had not taken him long to fall back into the feigned modes of conduct he despised. Showing enthusiasm when he had none came easier to him than he thought.

“I wanted to introduce you to Mr. Fellows,” Miss Smythe said, fluttering her lashes, which appeared to be a nervous habit as opposed to a means of flirtation.

“Mr. Fellows?” He made an attempt to look interested.

“My friend Jayne’s brother. Do you not remember me telling you that he has recently returned from a spell in India?”

She could well have mentioned it amongst all the talk of bonnets and bombazine. “Of course,” he lied.

Miss Smythe gestured to the gentleman with wavy black hair and ridiculous side-whiskers who, upon catching their eye, nodded to the row of chairs at the front.

“Oh, there he is.” In her excitement, Miss Smythe hopped about like a bird on a perch. “He did say we should all sit together.”

Tristan cleared his throat. “I prefer to sit at the back. I find one can appreciate the melody much more when it is carried through the room.”

Miss Smythe’s bright smile faded. “Oh. But Mr. Fellows is

here alone, and it would be rude not to accompany him now he has gone to the trouble of securing the best seats."

Tristan suppressed a smile. "You and Miss Hamilton may sit with Mr. Fellows. I shall sit elsewhere. Besides, I find Haydn can best be appreciated when there are no pretty distractions."

The lady blushed. "Well, if you're sure you don't mind."

"Not at all." He inclined his head. "And poor Mr. Fellows looks as though he could do with some company. Now, make haste before someone attempts to steal the seats from under his nose."

Miss Smythe gasped at the suggestion. "Shall we all meet for refreshments in the interval?"

"Certainly," he said with an affected smile.

Tristan watched them hurry away before heading to the empty row at the back. Dropping down into the chair, he gazed over the sea of heads and stifled a yawn.

Good Lord.

What the hell was he doing? With each passing day, he lost sight of the man who spied on smugglers, got drunk on cheap wine, cursed and laughed with labourers and farmhands. He hated behaving like a preened prig. Had his mother not been so distraught over the death of his brother, they would be sharing a few stern words

Tristan closed his eyes, but the low hum of mumbled whispers from the crowd, interspersed with a few strained chords of the cello, proved too distracting. He peered between the rows of shoulders to see Miss Smythe seated next to Mr. Fellows. Perhaps the gentleman had developed an affection for her. Tristan sincerely hoped so as it would ease his burden a little.

As the musicians began to play and the haunting notes filled the air, a sudden shiver raced through his body. Having chosen not to sit next to the aisle—if he fell asleep there was a good chance he would end up on the floor—he was surprised to find that the latecomer had decided to sit next to him as opposed to the empty row adjacent.

For fear of appearing rude he did not gape but glanced covertly out of the corner of his eye. The lady was dressed in grey silk, the edges of her sleeves trimmed with black lace. She held her hands demurely in her lap. The sight of her black gloves coupled with her sombre-looking gown complemented his own choice of black attire.

The lady edged a little closer. The air around them vibrated with a nervous energy that had nothing to do with the music. The hairs at his nape stood to attention, his body growing more acutely aware of the woman seated at his side. He shuffled back in the chair in an attempt to study her profile. But without any warning, she spoke.

"Hello, Tristan." Her words were but a soft purr. The soothing sound caused tingles to spark suddenly in various parts of his body, like fireworks shooting and bursting sporadically in the night sky.

He would know her voice anywhere.

He had heard it in his dreams too many times to forget its sweet timbre.

Turning slowly in a bid to prepare his weak heart, he glanced at her face. Her deep pink lips were just as full as he remembered. Her dark brown eyes still held the power to reach into his soul. The ebony curls were just as dark as the night he had covered her body with his own to claim the only woman he had ever wanted.

"Isabella." Years of torturous agony hung within that one word, years of longing, years of living with her betrayal.

"I must speak to you," she said, her breath coming as quick as his.

He suppressed a snigger of contempt. She'd had nothing to say to him when she left him and married another man. During the five years since their separation, she could have written to him many times. She could have found him in France if that was what she'd wanted.

Why here? Why now?

"After all this time, I doubt there is anything left to say." His tone was deliberately cold, blunt. The memories of her were like painful wounds that refused to heal and so he had no choice but to hide them beneath bandages of indifference.

"I did not come here for the music," she whispered, but he noted anger infused her tone.

What the hell did she have to be angry about?

The gentleman in front turned his head. "Shush."

Tristan cast him an irate glare. "And I did not come here to revisit the past," he muttered to her through gritted teeth.

"But this is not about the past." She gave a weary sigh as though she would rather be anywhere else than sitting talking to him. "This is about Andrew."

"Andrew?" He could not hide his surprise.

During the two months since his return, she had not called at the house. She had not come to pay her respects, or offer her condolences.

"I cannot speak about it here," she said as she placed a hesitant hand on his arm. His traitorous body responded immediately as a familiar warmth travelled through him. "My carriage is waiting outside."

Without another word, she stood and walked out through the door.

His heart lurched. The urge to run after her would never leave him.

He should tell her to go to the devil, let her husband be the one to listen to her pitiful woes. Turning back to face the musicians, he closed his eyes in the hope the melody would ease his restless soul. But the haunting harmony only served to remind him of all he had lost.

Perhaps if he went to her, she would offer an explanation for her lies and deceit. Perhaps then he would be able to move forward, take a wife, and produce an heir.

Straightening his coat as he stood, he crept out of the room.

When it came to Isabella, he would always be too weak to resist.

Books by Adele Clee

To Save a Sinner

A Curse of the Heart

What Every Lord Wants

The Secret To Your Surrender

A Simple Case of Seduction

Anything for Love Series

What You Desire

What You Propose

What You Deserve

What You Promised

The Brotherhood Series

Lost to the Night

Slave to the Night

Abandoned to the Night

Lured to the Night

Lost Ladies of London

The Mysterious Miss Flint

The Deceptive Lady Darby

The Scandalous Lady Sandford

The Daring Miss Darcy

Avenging Lords

At Last the Rogue Returns

Printed in Great Britain
by Amazon

86688199R00132